Gordon Kirkland

MW00940612

The Night Before Christmas

Other Books by Gordon Kirkland

Humor Essays

- *Justice Is Blind – And Her Dog Just Peed In My Cornflakes[1]*
- *Never Stand Behind A Loaded Horse[2]*
- *When My Mind Wanders It Brings Back Souvenirs[3]*
- *I Think I'm Having One Of Those Decades*
- *I May Be Big But I Didn't Cause That Solar Eclipse*
- *Holly Jolly Frivolity*

Novels

- *Crossbow*

---

[1] Winner, 2000 Stephen Leacock Award of Merit For Humour
[2] Winner, 2005 Stephen Leacock Award of Merit For Humour
[3] Winner, 2006 Stephen Leacock Award of Merit For Humour

The Plight Before Christmas

Gordon Kirkland

At Large Publishing
Pitt Meadows, BC, Canada

ISBN-13: 978-1461188988
ISBN-10: 1461188989

To Diane, Mike, Brad & Deb
Who make it all worthwhile.

And

To my brother Jim, and my sister Lois
who shared many a holiday disaster with
me during our childhood.

Special Thanks To:

Tracy Beckerman & Bruce Cameron

The Plight Before Christmas

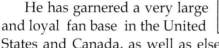*Gordon Kirkland* is a three-time recipient of the Stephen Leacock Award of Merit as a finalist for the Leacock Medal for his collections of humorous essays.

He has garnered a very large and loyal fan base in the United States and Canada, as well as elsewhere around the world.

Gordon Kirkland has been a workshop leader and keynote speaker at dozens of writer's conferences, festivals, and university programs over the past fifteen years. This includes three sessions of the University of Dayton's Erma Bombeck Writer's Workshop, six years on the faculty of the Southern California Writer's Conference, as well as many more. He has lectured at Simon Fraser University (Vancouver, BC), Ball State University (Muncie, Indiana), The University of Georgia (Athens, GA), and Florida First Coast Community College (Jacksonville, FL.)

In 2009, Kirkland was one of the stars of *The 3-Day Novel*, a television series on Canada's BookTelevision, in which 12 Canadian writers were locked in a large bookstore with the task of writing a full novel in just 72 hours. This was carried out under the watchful eye of television cameras, store customers, and with numerous interruptions aimed at breaking the writers' trains of thought.

Gordon lives near Vancouver, BC with, Diane, and their adopted Labrador Retriever, Tara. They have two grown sons.

The Plight Before Christmas

Contents

Forward

The Plight Before Christmas

The holiday season has always been a source of trepidation for me. There have been a variety of disasters, accidents, calamities, and misadventures that have befallen me, and/or members of my family during the season of joy and good will toward men. They may have been as benign as discovering that many of the light bulbs that all lit up when the string of lights was on the ground, were blown by the time I got them hung around the eaves, or as problematic as being snowed under in a holiday blizzard.

Many of those events have been adapted for this story and, as fiction allows, embellished somewhat to draw out the full extent of the question every author must ask, "*What if?*"

What if things went a bit further than they actually did?

What if Santa Claus didn't really bring the gifts,

but made the people who do the shopping understand the importance of the wishes of a young boy?

What if a trip home from the dentist's during a blizzard led to a serious jumping to premature confusions at the sight of an unconscious mother?

What if a snow plow driver took more joy filling in people's driveways and burying their cars than actually clearing the streets?

It all adds up to the plight before Christmas.

Chapter One

A Hard Time To Feel Joyous

James Kelly looked out the window of his store, and sighed. The winter sky looked gray and foreboding, but the thermometer suggested that even if precipitation was going to drop from those clouds, it was probably just going to be more rain.

"It would only need to go down a couple of degrees to make it snow," he thought, but he knew that the forecast was calling for more days with temperatures above freezing in the week ahead.

James had seen just about all the rain he could take and the prospect of more was depressing. Here it was, December seventeenth and there hadn't even been a hint of snow. James needed snow to get him into the holiday spirit, and on this particular year, he needed to feel the holiday spirit more than any in recent memory.

The lack of snow had apparently affected the Christmas shoppers as well. There had not been the sudden post-Thanksgiving rush that he had seen in other years. Like most shopkeepers, he depended on those sales for a good percentage of his annual income.

The business wasn't doing well. He'd stuck to his belief that children still wanted toys to capture their imagination, but the computer and video games that he abhorred had long since taken over the market. Children would rather sit with a televised image of a car race than with an actual car race set. Reality had given way to the imaginary.

It just didn't require real imagination.

For years, he had depended on the fathers who, like him, remembered the joy of playing with an electric train or car race and wanted to share that feeling with their own sons. Often fathers came in to buy an electric train when their sons were still babies, rationalizing that they would enjoy watching the train go around the track circuit, while the dads manned the controls. Grown men were reliving their childhood joys through the eyes of their sons.

Now the first wave of the video game generation was becoming fathers and his sales were suffering for it.

"One more really good Christmas season is all that I need. I could sell the store in the New Year, and retire," he said, although he wasn't entirely sure if he was talking to himself or to the clouds that he hoped would soon start producing snow.

"What's that?"

James had forgotten about Jill, who was working in the back sorting through the inventory. He touched his sports coat and felt the envelope in his pocket, the one that contained the paperwork needed to let Jill go. He hated the thought of firing her right before Christmas, but the store's sales could barely sustain him. The luxury of having a staff person around the store was one he was going to have to forego. He had been delaying the inevitable, but the letter that he received from the bank the day before was forcing his hand. It would have to be done today, but he decided to let it slide for a couple more hours.

"Just wishing for some snow," he said. "I didn't realize I was wishing out loud."

"We all are," Jill called from the back. "My kids are afraid Santa won't come without snow."

James winced at the mention of her children. She barely made the minimum wage, and he wondered how losing her job would affect them. He didn't have to wonder for long. An old, almost forgotten memory jumped out of the recesses of his mind and filled his thoughts with the knowledge of exactly how it would affect them.

He walked back to the tiny office in the rear of the store, and rifled through the envelopes the postman had delivered. There were no surprises; just more bills.

"I'm going over to Marie's for a bite," James said. "Do you want anything?"

"No," Jill replied. "I brought my usual."

Jill's usual was a container of thin chicken noodle soup, and a small bag of soda crackers. She saved bread and peanut butter for her sons' lunches.

James got up from his desk and pulled on his coat for the short walk across the street to the diner for lunch. Even though the temperature was above freezing, the wind made it feel much colder. It had stripped all of the leaves from the trees and was blowing them in little tornadoes along the street.

He spent more time staring at the food on his plate than he did eating it. He could never recall feeling so far down in the dumps. He watched with some feigned interest as Marie, the owner of the diner, started hanging decorations around the mirror behind the counter.

She was suffering too. The corporate coffee shops had arrived in town with their egg nog flavored cappuccinos and lattes. Customers had moved on, willing to spend three times as much for a trendy coffee than the good old bottomless cup at Marie's.

"Maybe if we pretend it looks like Christmas the snow will follow," Marie suggested.

"Maybe we should all stand out in the middle of the street singing *Let It Snow*," said James trying hard to sound like he was in a better mood than he really was.

Marie filled a cup and put it down in front of James. She filled a second one for herself. and sat down beside him.

"You look lower than your usual morose self," she said.

James normally kept most things bottled up inside him, both at home and at work, but the pressure he was feeling got the better of him.

"It looks like I have to let Jill go today," he said staring at the steam rising from his coffee. "You know what business is like around here. No one comes downtown anymore. They'd rather all stop at that monstrosity of a mall out by the highway. I guess I can't blame them, really. With indoor parking, Santa's Castle, and roving bands of carolers wandering the mall is a lot more pleasant than wandering around down here in the rain. When Clarkson's Department Store closed up here and moved out there, they took the main reason people had for coming downtown with them."

"Can't it wait until the new year, at least?" Marie asked, touching James on the arm. "You know she has two little kids and all."

"I don't see how." James said, still staring at his coffee. "The bank is really putting the screws to me."

The rain had started before James left the diner. The wind driven drops seemed to bite into his cheeks as he made his way back to his shop. Just as he was digging in his pocket for the keys, a single snowflake descended in front of him. He looked at the clouds hoping to see more, but just filled his eyes with cold rain.

"OK," he said, "now you're just teasing me."

When James came back inside he went directly to his office and took off his overcoat. He touched his jacket pocket and felt the envelope. He sat down behind his desk, and called Jill.

He opened his desk drawer. Beside the bottle of scotch that had been squirreled away in there, was a small cash box. He opened it and counted the few bills he kept in there. With the scattering of coins it amounted to $89.37. He sighed and set the box on the corner of the desk. He reached for the bottle, then thought better of it and closed the drawer.

"You wanted to see me, boss," Jill said.

She was smiling, but her face couldn't hide the weight of her own worries.

"Yes. Jill," James started. "You have to know things aren't going so well around here…"

Jill nodded.

"…and the bank is getting really snarly with me, so I have to…"

James stopped, when his eyes focused on the cash box he had left on his desk. An idea shot through his mind and out of his mouth before he could even think of all the reasons why it was the wrong thing to do.

"I have to tell you that there isn't much for a Christmas bonus, this year, so I thought I'd give you something a little different. I'm going to raid the petty cash, and give you three extra weeks' vacation starting now, so you can spend the holidays with your kids."

He reached for the cash box and counted out seventy-five dollars, and handed it to Jill. She looked surprised.

"Well," she said, "that's certainly not what I was expecting. I thought you were calling me back here to let me go."

"With a little over a week to go before Christmas? What kind of a Scrooge do you take me for?" James said trying hard to make it look like that hadn't been the original plan. "And take one of those starter sets home to put under your tree. Your boys are old enough for a train set now."

James stood by the door as Jill left the store. He watched her walk across the street, and down the sidewalk. When she got to Marie's, the cafe owner came out with a large box; the kind she used to package up her pies when customers wanted to take the whole thing home for dessert. She gave the box to Jill. It was obvious that Marie was trying to cheer Jill up, thinking that James had let her go. The two women spoke for a minute, and a surprised look came over Marie's face. She stared across the street toward the store and saw James watching them. She gave him a questioning look, and all James could do was reply with a resigned shrug.

As James walked to the back of the store, he was startled to hear the door chime ring. A man about his age entered with a boy of about ten or eleven. The father looked at the train display. James flipped the switch at the back of the store and the display came to life.

"There," the father said to the son. "That's like the train I had when I was your age."

The boy looked bored.

"Do they have the Vidsystem 3 here?" he asked looking around the shop. "The new Game Center store at the mall has Vidsystem 3's. That's what I want for Christmas."

The father looked to James, who just shook his head sadly. The father looked saddened, as well. He tried to tell the son about the fun he had with his train set, but the boy was adamant. He let his father know in no uncertain terms that trains were not on his wish list, just the Vidsystem 3 and a variety of game cartridges for it. They left the store. James stood at the window and watched them head down the street to their car. As they did, a couple more snowflakes drifted down from the clouds.

"I said enough with the teasing." he said looking at the sky.

But the clouds weren't teasing. Slowly but surely more snowflakes joined the raindrops. As they increased in numbers, the raindrops began to fade into the background. Within a few minutes the snow had completely taken over.

The weatherman had been wrong, and James was more than a little bit pleased by the error.

He stood watching the snow. Across the street Marie was in her window looking at it, too. The flakes grew larger and increased in intensity. The wind eased up. It wasn't long before the snowflakes began to look like feathers floating down from some great flock of geese flying overhead.

As he watched, James began to remember another snowstorm that he had waited for many years before. Watching the snowflakes falling outside proved to be hypnotic and he started to daydream, remembering watching the snow fall from Miss Witherspoon's fourth grade classroom.

Chapter Two

Same Feeling / Different Time

On that distant day, the snow started falling early in the afternoon, taking with it the attention spans of the fourth graders. Heavy white flakes drifting down from the sky were far more interesting than phonics.

It was late this year. There were already rumors starting to spread through the halls and lunchroom that if it didn't snow soon, bad things were sure to start happening. No one wanted the prospect of a green Christmas, especially those who were anxiously awaiting the holiday season.

None   were   more   anxious   than   Miss

Witherspoon's fourth graders. They all knew that snow was a prerequisite for Christmas. No snow, no sleigh. No sleigh, no Santa. It was a simple concept, far easier to comprehend than the twelve times table that they knew they'd have to recite before they could leave for the day.

James looked out at the snow falling with a sense of relief. Much of that relief was due to the aforementioned need for snow so Santa could make his rounds. He had another reason to feel relieved, though; a much darker reason.

Snow at Christmas meant that people wouldn't be dying.

It was an odd thought for a ten-year-old boy, but it was the sort of thing that came naturally to James. Even his younger sister, who was down the hall in the second grade class, would be thinking the same thing when she looked out the window and saw the snow.

"A green Christmas and the graves will be full."

The Kelly kids had heard that saying a hundred times that year. As November ended without snow, it was heard more often. It was the first thing their Aunt Doris would say as she looked out the kitchen window sipping her tea in the morning. They'd hear her say it throughout the day.

When she'd stop by their bedrooms to say goodnight, she'd take another glance out the window. Seeing the grass still visible on the front lawn, she'd say it again. James and Louise would go to sleep thinking about the graveyard overflowing with bodies, and the worry that one of those bodies might belong to Santa Claus, who would surely die if he tried to land his sleigh where there was no snow to cushion the descent.

Their aunt, who was actually their mother's aunt and more like a grandmother to the children, didn't mean any harm by her pronouncement. She had been young at a time when a green Christmas meant that there might be more diseases around. In those days people died from the flu much more easily than they did now. The cold weather brought snow with it, and killed off some of the germs that caused the graves to fill.

It was just one of her many sayings. James thought those sayings were the reason that she had never gotten married. She probably scared off any potential husbands by saying things like "A green Christmas and the graves will be full."

James looked out the window at the snow with a sense of relief. Santa would be safe. Christmas would be saved. People wouldn't be dying.

More importantly, he might not have to listen to his aunt repeatedly telling him about the impending doom of complete strangers who would succumb to the dreaded Green-Chrismasitis.

It was the seventeenth of December. Christmas

was just eight days away. If the snow could just keep falling, they'd be riding their toboggans down the Hill of The Seven Bumps in the park down the street by the weekend.

School would be out for almost two weeks. It could snow every day as far as the children were concerned. Snow was synonymous with fun for a ten-year-old boy, even if it meant that he had to bring his seven-year-old sister along with him. At least they wouldn't have to bring Georgie along. At three, he was just too young to be left in the care of James and Louise. He'd have to stay home and sit in the kitchen with their mother and her aunt.

Fathers would soon be able to build skating rinks in their backyards. Children up and down Parkland Road could skate the day away. Hockey games would erupt in some yards. Figure skating championships would take place in others. It all depended on the gender of the oldest child.

Boy-controlled skating rinks were filled with shouts of "He shoots! He scores!"

Boys would pretend to be Gordie Howe, or Maurice Richard, skating down the ice hoping to drift the puck past some hapless goalie.

Girl controlled skating rinks were the home of imaginary Winter Olympics. Imaginations ran wild among the girls as they pretended to be Carol Heiss or Barbara Ann Scott skating before wildly cheering crowds.

James and Louise didn't have to worry about who would control the skating rink in their backyard. There wouldn't be one. Their father was not about to spend his time away from work standing in the yard freezing his fingers trying to spray water over a section of flattened snow.

"It'll ruin the lawn," he'd say whenever they asked if they could have a rink.

Ruining a lawn was one of the greatest sins in their father's mind. He was convinced that somehow Moses forgot to mention a commandment that said, "Thou shalt not ruin thy father's lawn."

If other kids' fathers wanted to breach that rule in their yards, let them. James and Louise could go skate on their rinks. He'd be the one with the better lawn next summer, and then those fathers would be sorry.

The snow was starting to build up on the ground. A couple of inches were already stacked up on the tops of the fence posts along the edge of the schoolyard. Soon the grass would completely disappear beneath the white blanket.

It had James' full attention. Watching the snow fall was far more interesting than listening to Miss Witherspoon drone on about the importance of phonics to a well-rounded education. James could care less at that point how many ways you could create the f-sound.

F, ph, and gh didn't play any part in the thoughts he was having about the fun, phun, ghun he'd have when the school bell rang and he could get out into that snow.

The snow intensified as the time dragged on.

Occasionally James would look at the clock to see how much longer it would be before he'd be free of Miss Witherspoon, and outside in all that fresh snow.

Time had slowed. It almost seemed to stand still. Each time he looked at the clock it would be just a few minutes since the last time. Seconds felt like minutes. Minutes felt like hours. The two hours that remained before the school day ended were going to take an eternity to pass.

Maybe it was just because it had been eight long months since he last saw snow falling, and eight months represented a long time in the life of a ten-year-old, but the flakes seemed bigger than any he had seen before. It almost looked like a flock of giant white geese were molting as they flew overhead. Perhaps it was Mother Nature's way of making up for lost time. She needed big flakes to get the snow cover caught up to where it should be by the seventeenth of December.

Those flakes mesmerized James. He stared out the window, completely oblivious to his surroundings. In his mind he was already outside, crafting the perfect snowball to throw at his sister's back. The snow seemed to be calling him, and laughing as it fell.

"James…"

"James…?"

"JAMES KELLY!"

He was startled when the snow shouted at him. It broke the trance. The snow wasn't calling his name. It was Miss Witherspoon. The laughter of the snowflakes was really the laughter of his classmates who were all looking at him.

"Do you know the answer, James," said Miss Witherspoon in that tone of hers that she used when she thought she had another candidate for chalkboard cleaning after school.

"Yes, Ma'am," James stammered, trying to remember what it was they had been studying.

"Well, we're all waiting," the teacher added.

"F, ph, and gh," said James, proud of himself for his quick recall under such stressful conditions.

"That's a fine answer," Miss Witherspoon said, over the laughter of the rest of the class. "Unfortunately, James, 'F, ph and gh' is not the correct answer to the question, 'What is twelve times nine.'"

James was crestfallen. He had daydreamed through the remainder of the phonics class and part way into arithmetic. He knew what was going to happen next, and he was uncannily accurate in his prediction; so accurate in fact, he mouthed the words along with Miss Witherspoon as she spoke them.

"Alright, James, after class, you will write the twelve times table on the board ten times. No, let's make that twelve times. That sounds so much more apropos. After I check your work, you will erase it all and then clean the dust from the chalkboard brushes. James, are you mocking me?"

A detention was bad enough on any normal day, but to have a detention on the day of the first snowfall, especially when that first snowfall had come so late in the year, was beyond being cruel and unusual punishment.

The day continued to drag on. The snow continued to build. By the time the school bell rang at three-thirty, almost six inches had fallen. The other children ran excitedly from the school, barely taking time to do up their coats. James could hear them shouting and laughing. He heard girls scream as boys' snowballs met their targets. He could almost taste the icy flakes on his tongue.

He stood at the board writing the twelve times table, under the watchful stare of Miss Witherspoon. When he was finished and had erased all remnants of the twenty minutes worth of work, he took the chalkboard erasers outside and began banging them together to clean them.

He pictured Miss Witherspoon's head between the erasers as he smacked them together. She had spoiled the first snowfall of the year for him.

The other kids were long gone from the schoolyard as James walked slowly home. He kicked at a small snowdrift. There was no point picking up any. His sister would already be at home. He was without a target. It almost made him wish the snow hadn't come at all.

He was the poster boy for the Society of Dejected Ten-Year-Olds.

"Christmas could be green and the graveyard full for all I care," he thought.

He was surprised when that thought made him smile. He wasn't smiling because of the thought of hordes of faceless strangers filling up the graves. He was picturing the graveyard filled with a lifeless

Miss Witherspoon. In James' mind, she was fat enough to fill the graveyard all by herself.

He pictured her ample posterior sticking through the ground in the graveyard because the workmen wouldn't be able to dig a hole big enough for her to fit. She'd be wearing her green Monday and Wednesday dress to blend in with the grass between the gravestones. Her purple Tuesday and Thursday dress with the orange stripes would be too much of a distraction for passing motorists, and her yellow Friday skirt with the red blouse was equally blinding.

He imagined what it would be like to see that sight after the first snow. Kids could probably toboggan down her butt. That thought made him laugh out loud.

He was still laughing to himself when he started up the driveway at home. That's when the snowball hit. It came from behind the tree on the Cooper's front lawn. It caught him perfectly behind his left ear and sent icy crystals running down his neck and inside his coat and shirt.

Anger welled up inside him. It wasn't the same anger he had felt when banging the chalk brushes together outside the school door. This was a disappointed anger.

Someone else had gotten in the first snowball before him.

He had dreamt about his first snowball of that year's campaign. He even thought about it in the middle of July up at the lake. He had planned how he would make the perfect orb between his mittens and throw it with just the right arc and intensity to catch Louise right where the snowball that was trickling down his ear canal had caught him. Now whoever it was hiding behind the Cooper's tree had done it first.

"Coop!" he shouted, convinced that it was his friend and occasional mortal enemy, Mike Cooper, who had knocked the image of Miss Witherspoon's butt/ski hill from his mind.

James picked up a handful of snow and started forming a ball. He didn't have time to pack it into anything remotely resembling the perfect snowball he had imagined all spring, summer and through the longest fall in memory. He knew that he was at a severe disadvantage. Whoever had launched that first missile had the advantage of time on his side. While James had been writing the twelve times table on the blackboard, every other kid in the neighborhood could have been preparing a stockpile of cold snowy weapons of icy destruction.

As he neared the tree, his adversary stepped out and launched a second attack. James was so shocked by the sight that he dropped his snowball.

The world seemed to be moving in slow motion. He saw the snowball leave the mittens of his foe. It watched it sail through the space between them, and stood frozen in time as it hit him just above the bridge of his nose. In the split second that passed from the launch to the impact, James was able to take in every detail of the scene in front of him. He could see the tree, the fresh snow all around him, the grin on the face of the perpetrator and the snowball from the time it those mittens.

Those pink mittens.

Those pink mittens his sister was wearing.

The knock on the window behind him took his attention away from his sister for a moment. Aunt Doris and Georgie were standing at the living room window laughing and clapping.

Aunt Doris opened the window and shouted, "Way to go, Louise. Just the way I showed you!"

"Just the way I showed you?" thought James. "Even Auntie Doris is out to get me today."

He didn't have long to think about the growing paranoia festering in his ten-year-old mind. Another snowball caught him just below the nape of his neck and trickled down his back. James didn't say anything. He walked slowly and dejectedly into the house, took off his coat and shoes and headed for his room.

The day had been ruined; this perfect day of all days; the day when snow finally arrived on Parkland Road; the day that should have been the pinnacle day of the kid year.

Ruined. Totally ruined.

As he lay on his bed, several words came to mind. They were the only words that could sum up his feelings about the past hour and a half. They were words that he knew better than to say aloud, because they were virtually guaranteed to result some in form of punishment that would further ruin his day.

He repeated the words over and over in his mind. Maybe if he repeated them to himself twelve times, or even twelve times twelve times, it would release the frustration of missing the first few minutes of play in the snow after school, and of being hit by his seven-year-old sister's perfectly made and fired snowball.

He desperately wanted to shout them out as

loudly as he could, just as he had heard his father do when he had hit his thumb with a hammer on the roof of the cottage last summer.

It wasn't even that they were the kind of words that he knew would result in a far greater punishment that he cared to imagine. They just weren't words that were supposed to be said in the Kelly household, especially if his mother was anywhere within earshot.

Lorraine Kelly preferred to use euphemisms for anything that she thought was at all disgusting or fit into the category of topics not to be discussed in the home. Some of the words made a bit of sense; others were made up and only known to members of the Kelly household.

One did not say that they were going to the toilet at the Kelly's. The preferred term was that you needed to visit the room where Lizzie Borden hid her axe. The thought always gave James a bit of a chill. He always half expected to see a blood encrusted axe hidden behind the door.

The bodily functions that one took care of in the room where Lizzie Borden hid her axe also had their own unique names.

If you were a Kelly child, you did not pee. You 'widdied.'

James did not know anyone else whose family used that term, and it had made for some embarrassing moments when he first announced he had to widdy on his first day of kindergarten.

Widdy was also the name of the part of the body from which widdy flowed.

That too caused embarrassing moments. Georgie had once greeted Reverend Armstrong with the announcement that when he brushed his teeth his widdy wiggled.

Cooper children did not poo or take a crap. They had a grunty. James strived with all his might to never use the word grunty in a public place.

None of the words that he was thinking, as he lay on his bed examining the unfairness of the day, fit into the category of appropriate euphemisms for members of the Kelly family.

James lay on his bed, with all the words he dared not say running through his mind. Words like 'damn' and 'crap' could have aptly described how he was feeling. Of course the classic word beginning with the letter F (or phonetically with a ph or gh as well) was so far off limits that he did his level best to avoid even thinking it.

"Damn it all," he thought. "This whole day has just been blown all to crap, when it should have been the f… ph… gh… finest first day of snow ever."

"I beg your pardon," called Aunt Doris from the hall.

James clasped his hand over his mouth realizing that somehow his thoughts had escaped from inside his brain where they were supposed to stay, and made their way to his vocal chords.

Chapter Three

The Other Side Of Joyous

James didn't have long to worry about his errant thoughts. Something even more disturbing was already making its way down Parkland Road; something he had forgotten about in the eight months since the last snowfall.

Snow, especially the first snowfall of the year might be a wonderful thing to a ten-year-old boy, but there are two sides to every coin. The flip side of this particular coin was waiting for James in the garage. It was heavy, ancient, and according to Aunt Doris, needed his immediate attention.

The family's old snow shovel.

James tried to ignore the sound as soon as he was able to identify it, but Aunt Doris knew only too well what the rumbling sound meant.

Steve Murphy was making his way down Parkland Road in the snowplow. He lived for nights like this. He dreamt about major snowstorms. They were the one thing that brought joy to his life.

To him, creating the huge drifts of snow along the side of the city's roads was an art. The streets belonged to him as he rode along high above the other vehicles in the plow's cab. Great arcs of snow billowed out from the edge of his plow. They were things of beauty to Steve.

One of the best parts of the job for Steve was watching the plow fill in the end of the driveways in the better parts of town. He knew he could wipe out an hour's work for some rich jerk with just a single pass of his plow.

To Steve, the better parts of town included anywhere outside the grounds of the trailer park where his aged singlewide occupied a corner near the back. Even a middle-class neighborhood like Parkland Road, was filled with rich jerks in Steve's mind. They all deserved to have the ends of their driveways filled in by the plume erupting from the end of his plow blade.

Steve was someone few people wanted to mess with. Everyone in town knew that when he was behind the wheel of the plow, it was best to stay out of his way. For that matter, it was best to stay out of his way period. If he was given the slightest reason to take a disliking to someone, that person would find his driveway plugged even after a short flurry.

Steve knew this was his one source of power. He'd swagger around the town and in the bars and taverns downtown wearing a t-shirt with the sleeves rolled up to better display his ornate tattoo. It featured a skeletal grim reaper, driving a snowplow, with great arcs of snow burying a parked car. Beneath it were the words, "Beware! The Plowman Cometh."

His anger and attitudes had been beaten into him. Between his father who shared the view that life was unfair because some people had more than he did, to the other kids he had gone to school with who derided him for his second hand clothes, Steve grew up to hate the world and most of its inhabitants. As a snow plow driver, he had a way to make their lives miserable, and he rarely missed a chance to enact revenge on the "rich jerks" of the town.

Steve saw James standing in the driveway staring at him. He adjusted the lever connected to the plow, which let the snow build up on the blade rather than distributing it evenly along the side of the road. When he got to the end of the Kelly driveway he pulled the lever again. A great wave of snow and ice arced in the air, and descended on James and the driveway. The lane was filled, and James was left looking like a snowman.

All of it would have to be removed before James' father could get the car into the driveway. That was James' job, and he didn't want to think about the mood his father would be in if he got home and found that it hadn't been done.

Slowly he made his way to the basement to find last year's galoshes. When he found them, he realized there was going to be a problem. His feet had grown two sizes over the summer. There was no way his running shoe was going to fit into the boot. His only choice was to go out into the snow wearing the galoshes over a pair of socks.

He knew that as soon as he told his parents that his boots no longer fit him his father would say, "You know you'd be a lot taller if you didn't have so much tucked under the bottom of your legs."

It was as predictable as hearing about the graves being full if there was a green Christmas. Anything to do with his feet or shoes would make his father make that comment.

"Like I can do anything about it," thought James. "Maybe he'd seem a lot taller if he still had some hair on top of his head."

That thought made him smile. He briefly thought about saying that the next time his father said anything about how much he had tucked under his legs. He kept that thought brief. His father was not the sort of man who took comments about his hair loss with a sense of humor, especially if the comment came from a ten-year-old.

James was surprised when he pushed open the side door. The snow hadn't stopped falling and the flakes still looked like goose feathers drifting down from the sky. Where there had been ten inches of snow when he walked into the house after the humiliation of his sister's snowball attack, there was now well over a foot.

Mother Nature was making up for lost time.

He walked across the lane to the small building that served as the garage and tool shed to retrieve the shovel. As he did he felt the cold penetrate through the thin rubber of his galoshes. They might have been fine if his shoe had fit in there, but they provided no warmth over a pair of socks, even the hand-knit scratchy wool ones his aunt made for him every year.

James attacked the pile that the plow had left at the end of the driveway first. It was nearly three feet deep and filled the first fifteen feet of the lane. As he dug, he let his imagination distract him from the snow. Instead of a ten-year-old boy with a snow shovel, he became a prospector digging for gold. He pretended to have the taste of moonshine whiskey in his mouth. He had no idea what that might taste like, but he assumed it had to be better than broccoli.

He dug into the pile, searching for the mother lode. It had to be there somewhere. When he finally managed to get a small trench dug down to the cement of the sidewalk, it became his imaginary vein of gold.

"Gold!" he shouted. "I've found gold!"

He took a long swig from his imaginary jug of moonshine to celebrate his newfound wealth. He was oblivious to the sight of his aunt watching him through the living room window, unsure about her nephew's behavior.

"There's something wrong with that boy," she muttered as she shook her head and walked back to the warmth of the kitchen.

James worked on that pile for over half an hour, slowly but surely uncovering the sidewalk that, in his imagination, had become the world's largest vein of pure gold.

When that was done, he started to clear the rest of the driveway. The snow was piled up over the tops of his boots. He had to be careful where he stepped, because he didn't want the snow to cascade down the inside of his galoshes, the way it had run down his back after his sister's unprovoked act of aggression.

The going was slow as he worked his way up the driveway. He didn't go too deep, because he didn't want to hit the gravel surface and throw stones onto the lawn with the snow. His father had drilled that into him. Gravel was to stay on the driveway at all costs.

"Thou shalt not cause your father to hit a stone with the lawnmower," was another one of those commandments Moses had forgotten to tell the children of Israel after he came down from the mountain. The children of Charles knew better.

James concentrated more on the job ahead of him. It was dark out now, and his father would be home from work soon. James knew that it would be in his own best interest to have the driveway completely cleared before his dad pulled the old Ford into the driveway.

After well over an hour of work, he was almost completed. James' feet ached in the cold galoshes. His arms burned from the exertion of clearing the fifty-foot long driveway. He threw the last few shovelfuls onto the yard, and walked to the house.

He was cold, tired and hungry. He knew that dinner wouldn't be served until his parents got home. He hoped that after all that work he might be able to convince Aunt Doris to give him a couple of cookies and maybe even a mug of hot cocoa.

When he slid his galoshes off, his socks stayed inside. His feet were bright red and cold. He pulled off his coat and snow pants and sat down with his feet by the radiator to try to warm them up. He tried to remember why he had been so excited to see the snow. It seemed that ever since it had arrived, it had caused him nothing but trouble.

That wasn't about to change.

The warmth from the radiator had just started to cut through the cold of James' feet when he heard the sound again.

That unmistakable sound.

A steady rumble, mixed with a scraping, lots of metallic banging, and the rattle of chains. It was a sound that could rival any ghoul or ghost that a young boy's imagination could conjure. It was a sound that made James' heart sink to the bottom of his still icy feet.

Steve Murphy was making another pass down Parkland Road.

James ran to look through the window on the side door, hoping beyond hope that his father had managed to beat the snowplow. He prayed that he'd see some sign that the car had just pulled into the garage. He knew before he even looked that with the way his afternoon had gone thus far, the chances that he would see tire tracks in the fresh snow in the driveway were about as remote as the chances of Miss Witherspoon fitting into a size ten dress.

James turned and started walking up the stairs to his room to get a couple of dry pairs of socks. He needed to find another pair of mittens, because the ones he had worn earlier were soaking wet and lying on the radiator near the front door.

"Is that the snowplow I hear?" called Aunt Doris. "You'll have to clear the end of the driveway again before your father can get into the garage."

"The woman has an acute sense of the obvious," thought James. "Too bad she doesn't have the sense not to send me back out into the storm."

He could hear his sister playing in her room as he went past it. She didn't have to shovel snow or do any of the hard chores around here. James felt that the world was just not fair to ten-year-olds. They have to do all the hard work and they don't get any recognition for their efforts. He might as well be a slave.

James pictured the scene of himself dressed in thin clothes, barefoot and wearing shackles around his legs, as he stood knee-deep in snow trying to clear the driveway. His sister and Georgie would be watching through the window sipping cups of hot cocoa and eating chocolate chip cookies. Miss Witherspoon would be behind him cracking a whip and telling him to get a move on. Wolves, smelling his blood circled in the background waiting to carry him off if he succumbed to the cold and the lack of nourishment that even one chocolate chip cookie could have prevented. Aunt Doris' voice droned on in the background.

"The plow went by again, James."

"Better get out there and shovel it again, James."

"JAMES EDWARD KELLY I AM TALKING TO YOU!"

Her sharp tone snapped James out of his daydream. He was no longer the poor tired, hungry and dejected slave being sent out into the cold to shovel the driveway. He was just a tired, hungry and dejected ten-year-old boy being sent out into the cold to shovel the driveway.

"Yes, Aunt Doris," he called. "I'm just looking for some dry mitts."

There was the answer to his problems. Surely, his aunt wouldn't send him out into the cold to shovel the snow if he couldn't find dry mitts. People who went out with wet mitts would "catch their death." He's heard her say that a hundred times or more.

James went downstairs and casually lifted a cookie from the pan that was cooling beside the oven.

"I guess I can't do it," he said. I don't have any dry mitts and I wouldn't want to catch my death."

Aunt Doris would have none of that.

"Here," she said, "Wear these."

She handed him a pair of his mother's mitts; the pair that matched Louise's. Aunt Doris was actually expecting a self-respecting ten-year-old boy to go outside, where he could be seen by the entire world, wearing bright pink mittens.

Had she lost her mind?

"No f-f-f-f-f-f...." started James, before catching himself and quickly running through a list of options that would not result in an oral encounter with the bar of soap.

"...f-f-for crying out loud!" he shrieked. "I can't go outside in pink mittens. What if Coop saw me?"

"Well, if Coop is any kind of a decent young man, and I'm not suggesting that he is or he isn't," said Aunt Doris, who was not all that keen on James' friend and sometimes mortal enemy, "then he'll understand that you are helping your family by keeping your driveway clear, no matter what you are wearing."

James knew the taste of defeat. It was almost as foul as the taste of soap. He knew that there was no sense arguing with his aunt. It was unlikely that she had ever lost a single argument in her entire life. Besides, he knew he could keep Coop silent if he had to.

He took his mother's mitts, pulled on his coat and snow pants, slid his double-socked feet into his galoshes, and headed for the garage to retrieve the snow shovel.

He looked at the wall of snow that the plow had left behind in the driveway. It seemed even bigger than the one that he had faced just a couple of hours earlier. He thought there had to be an easier way to get rid of it. Shoveling took too long.

He remembered a scene from one of his Superman comic books. The Man of Steel had been faced with a giant wall of ice moving towards Metropolis. He saved the day by melting it with his x-ray vision.

James stared at the snow. He glared at it. If only he had x-ray vision, he could take care of all the snow in everyone's driveway on Parkland Road. He'd be a hero to the entire neighborhood. His stare didn't seem to be having the desired effect. He heard the side door open.

"Aunt Doris says that the snow isn't going to shovel itself, James, and you'd better get to work before Daddy comes home."

It was Louise. She was using that singsong voice of hers that she used when passing on orders from their parents or Aunt Doris. James turned and stuck his tongue out at her, before walking to the end of the driveway to take on the task left behind by the plow.

He forgot about his imaginary vein of gold that had been beneath the pile earlier. This time he decided that he was a gravedigger.

"All right men," he shouted. We have a lot of work to do today. It's supposed to be a green Christmas and you know what that means. The graves are going to be full. Let's get at it. We have to dig a big one first, and it's going to take all of us to get the job done. Old Fatty Miss Witherspoon died last night after she choked on a sandwich made with a whole pig."

"Something's just not right with that boy," Aunt Doris muttered again as she turned away from the living room window. "He talks to himself too much. It just ain't healthy."

James kept digging. The snow hadn't let up a bit since it started. If anything it was snowing harder now than it had been earlier. The flakes weren't as big as they once were but there seemed to be a lot more of them. Visibility was reduced. He could just make out the lights in front of the church at the end of the next block.

Snow has a way of deadening all the softer sounds around a person. As a result, James didn't hear someone approaching him from behind.

"Hi James." said a voice, snapping him back to reality just as he was widening the grave for Miss

Witherspoon's ample body.

James jumped and turned around quickly. Standing behind him was his friend and sometimes mortal enemy, Coop. At least James was pretty sure it was Coop. It looked like Coop's coat and snow pants, but he had a scarf wrapped around his face so that only his eyes weren't covered.

"Nice mittens." he said.

James had forgotten about the color of his mother's mittens. He quickly thrust his hands into his pockets to hide them.

"They're my Mom's," he said. "Mine got wet the first time I was out here shoveling."

"Sure they are," mocked Coop.

James wasn't in the mood for Coop to be taking on the mortal enemy role just then. He picked up a handful of snow, packed it and sent the missile towards Coop's scarf encased head before the boy had a chance to run away. James prided himself in how fast he could make and launch a snowball. With the exception of the skirmish earlier in the day with his sister, James had rarely been beaten to the draw.

"Aaargh!" cried Coop, running towards his yard. "I've been hit with snow coming from pink mittens. I'm going to die. Nothing is worse than being hit with snow from pink mittens. Just ask the kid I saw get hit by his sister who was hiding behind my tree this afternoon. I bet he knows how bad pink mitten snow is. I bet he'll be sorry tomorrow that he got hit with pink mitten snow when I tell all the guys at school about him getting ambushed by a seven-year-old girl!"

"You do and I'll tell your sister what you did

with her bra!" shouted James.

Coop stopped dead in his tracks. James had held that threat over him for months. Every time Coop thought had something to tease James about, he'd bring up the case of the odd smelling training bra.

Coop had taken the bra from the clothesline that hung in their back yard and tied it to two tree branches down by the river. The boys used it to launch frog astronauts over the water. When they tired of that game, he hung the bra back on the clothesline as though nothing had happened. James and Coop nearly passed milk through their noses when they were sitting at the Cooper's kitchen table and saw Mary go outside in her housecoat, take the bra from the line and go upstairs to get dressed.

"My bra smells funny," Mary said to her mother.

Once again, the boys had trouble keeping their milk from entering their sinuses. If Mary had any idea what had happened to her bra that day, Coop would have faced very severe consequences, both from his sister and his parents. As a result, James knew it was the perfect thing to use to keep Coop in line whenever he thought he might have something over James.

Coop knew he was not going to be able to say anything about the pink mittens, so he headed for home and safety from James aim with a snowball.

James started walking up the driveway with the shovel, having finished clearing the damage left behind by the snowplow. The snow continued to fall, and he had a pretty good idea that his snow shoveling was far from over for the day.

As he set the shovel against the garage wall, the snow that had built up on the roof gave way and cascaded down onto the driveway in an avalanche. It left a pile nearly three feet deep in front of the garage door. James didn't have to wait to hear Aunt Doris tell him that he had better shovel it all away. He just started digging.

"I'm going to ask Santa for Superman's flame throwing vision."

Chapter Four

More Like The Unfair Season

The concept of Santa Claus was beginning to gnaw at James' subconscious. He had heard some of the older kids at school saying that Santa didn't exist. They said your parents placed gifts under your Christmas tree.

James wanted to believe in Santa Claus. There just seemed to be a growing stack of evidence against him. How could Santa visit all of the houses in the world in just one night and still have time to drop of presents at each of them? How could eight reindeer pull a sleigh packed with enough presents for everyone in the world?

How could Santa deliver a complete electric train set next door at Coop's house and just leave a couple of small things for James, Louise, and Georgie? James knew that he had been in a lot less trouble than Coop.

At least *he* hadn't set fire to his parents' garage with a badly aimed firework.

James tried to put those thoughts out of his mind while he finished shoveling the snow away from the garage door. He had other things to occupy his mind.

The one that was bothering him the most was the fact that his mother was not at home. His mother was always there when he got home from school. It was getting close to suppertime and she still hadn't returned from wherever she had gone that day.

It just wasn't like her.

The snow was still falling when James entered the house. He knew that the odds were pretty good that the plow would make another pass down Parkland Road before too long. He just hoped it would be after his father had gotten home. Maybe, if he noticed how much work James had already done with the snow shovel, he would go out and do it himself.

Aunt Doris had the radio on in the kitchen. She was listening to the news. She never missed the 5:45 news on the radio. James couldn't understand why she listened to it, because the newscaster made her angry with so many of his comments and opinions. He was talking about the storm and how many accidents had happened in the rush-hour traffic. James hoped that his parents weren't participants in any of them. The newscaster said it could be the worst snowstorm to hit the city in over thirty years.

Aunt Doris suggested that James sit down at the kitchen table with his brother and sister and she would serve them dinner. That really worried James. The evening meal was never served until everyone was home. Even on nights when his father was caught in a traffic jam, the family had waited until he got there before eating.

"Where's Mom," asked James.

"She went to the dentist to have a wisdom tooth pulled," replied his aunt. "Your father was supposed to pick her up after work. I guess the storm has slowed them down."

James and the younger children ate their macaroni and cheese quietly. They knew better than to make noise when their aunt was listening to the news. It could make her miss something the newscaster might say to make her angry.

"That man doesn't know his keester from a hole in the ground," she'd say two or three times during every newscast, but nothing could make her miss the opportunity.

Some nights she would even talk to the disembodied voice coming from the crackly radio speaker. James always thought that the newscaster should be thankful that he couldn't hear what Aunt Doris thought of him.

After dinner, James went upstairs to do his

homework. After writing the twelve times table out on the blackboard twelve times that afternoon after the rest of the children had gone out to play in the new snow, he thought it was completely unfair that he should have to do it again in his workbook for homework. He hadn't bothered to make his feelings known to Miss Witherspoon. He knew that just might make her double his workload.

It wasn't worth the risk.

He was working on his spelling list when he heard the telephone ring. He closed his book and went to the place at the top of the stairs that he called his listening post. He could sit there and hear what was going on downstairs without being seen by the adults. The listening post had served him well. That's how he had known that his mother was on her way to the hospital to have Georgie, even though his father had told him and Louise that they were going out to see a man about a dog.

His sister was still disappointed that they didn't come home with a dog.

Sitting at the listening post, James could hear one side of the conversation his aunt was having.

"Oh, Charles, I was starting to get worried about you in this storm. I've fed the children, and James has cleared the driveway twice. Where are you?"

"Where?"

"What on Earth are you doing there?"

"You've been what?"

"What for?"

"Where is Lorraine?"

"They've taken her where?"

James was beginning to wish that he had Superman's hearing as well as the x-ray vision. He wasn't getting enough information from his aunt's side of the conversation. The only thing he was sure of was that something very unusual was going on.

"OK, I'll call John and get him to come down there. Don't worry dear. I'm sure everything will work out fine."

James heard his aunt put the telephone receiver back on the hook. He expected to hear her dial his Uncle John's number. At least then, he would be able to find out what his father had been saying.

Uncle John was tall and thin. He was the brother of James' mother. He was a very precise man, who did all things in a slow deliberate manner. That included talking. It seemed to take forever for Uncle John to finish a simple sentence. He was married to Aunt Millicent. It was a good fit for both of them. James' mother said it took Aunt Millicent forever to understand a simple sentence.

Millicent rubbed James' mother the wrong way. James couldn't recall a time that his mother had dealt with his aunt that he didn't hear his exasperated mother say, "Oh! That woman."

She would often tell James that he should

"always remember, dear, you are only related to *that woman* by marriage." It was her way of making sure he didn't consider his aunt part of the family. She belonged to someone else's family, and as far as his mother was concerned, they were hanging out in trees somewhere in Africa.

James didn't hear Aunt Doris dialing. He heard his aunt clear her throat a couple of times, followed by a snort. What started quietly quickly built into a crescendo. Aunt Doris was laughing hysterically. She had a laugh that could almost shake the house. He could picture her sitting in the living room beside the telephone, her face reddened by the exertion of expelling a lengthy series of guffaws, snorts and giggles. James was pretty sure that, whatever it was that she was laughing at, his father would not appreciate it. He did not share his wife or her aunt's sense of humor. He especially disliked it when he was the cause of their laughter.

After several minutes, James heard the sound of his aunt clear her throat and begin dialing the telephone number for his Uncle John.

"John, you're not going to believe what has happened," she said.

"I have to whisper, because I don't want the children to hear me."

"Charles needs you to go down and meet him at the police station. He's been arrested"

James couldn't believe what he had just heard. Luckily, he had time to let the thought sink in without missing anything his aunt was saying. Uncle John was probable taking a few minutes to ask Aunt Doris what she meant.

"Lorraine was taken to the hospital. She's unconscious. The police think Charles knocked her out."

This was just too weird for James. He could never imagine his father raising his hand to his mother. He could well imagine, remember for that matter, his father raising his hand to give a spanking, but not to his mother. Everyone in the family revered James' mother, and his father was the chief worshiper in that department.

"I know it's snowing, John," his aunt was saying, but you need to go and bail Charles out so he can get to Lorraine."

"Of course he didn't." she said, after a lengthy pause, while his uncle had put the words together to question whether or not James' father might be guilty.

"She was at the dentist. It's a long story. Charles can tell you when you pick him up."

James was concerned. The speed at which Uncle John did things meant that his father could be stuck in a cell in the police station until the next day or even longer. That would definitely put a damper on Christmas, especially if the older kids at school were right about what they had been saying about Santa Claus being your parents.

James went downstairs to the kitchen and tried to appear as casual as he could in the circumstances.

"I just came down to sharpen a pencil. I'm doing

my homework. Yep, that's what I'm doing, just writing out the old twelve times table and doing my spelling," he said trying his hardest to let on that he didn't know what was going on.

"Who phoned?" he asked.

"Your father," said Aunt Doris. "He and your mother are going to be a little late."

"What are they doing?" he asked, just to see how his aunt would handle that one.

"Christmas shopping," she replied.

James was shocked. His aunt actually lied to him. He knew where his parents were, and she told a barefaced lie about it. To make matters worse it was a Christmas lie. You just didn't lie about anything to do with Christmas if you wanted to have Santa visit your house that year.

As he walked back upstairs, his aunt called to him, "When you've finished your homework, you'd better go back outside and clear the driveway again. Another four inches of snow has already fallen and the news says we can expect up to twelve more overnight. You don't want your father coming home to a driveway full of snow. You know how stressed he gets when he has to go shopping."

"She did it again," thought James.

His aunt was determined to lie to him about where his parents were. It made him wonder if she had lied to him about other things. Did Santa really bring nice warm socks for the good children who knew how to appreciate all the hard work that went into making them? She'd told him that enough times. Maybe it was a lie, too.

She'd say, "Toys and candy don't last too long,

but your feet have to last a lifetime. You'll appreciate having received warm socks when you are older and you haven't lost a toe or five to frostbite."

"I could appreciate a Clarkson's' Deluxe train set that would keep me inside out of the cold and prevent frostbite taking my toes, too," James would think whenever his aunt would extol the benefits of warm socks as Christmas gifts, but he knew better than to say it aloud.

Coop had been the recipient of a Clarkson's' train set last Christmas, making him the envy of most of the boys in Miss Witherspoon's class. It came mounted on a table in the basement. There were bridges, a tunnel, and all sorts of buildings. The train even whistled whenever it came close to one of the roads that were painted on the table. There were cars, people, and lights. The train had six cars behind the engine, including a coal car, a log car that actually dumped the logs when it was stopped by the lumber mill on the far side of the table, a refrigerated car that had miniature milk cans loaded inside it, a mail car, and two box cars with doors that opened so that cargo could be loaded inside.

That train kept Coop free of frostbitten toes.

Of course, Coop also benefited from his father, who owned the local Ford dealership, and could have their driveway plowed by the guy who plowed out the car lot after and during each snowstorm.

When James finished his homework, he went to

the living room and turned on the television. Big Top Circus was going to come on in a few minutes. Each week, James and Louise would tell Georgie that he could sit up close to the television to watch cartoons, just before Big Top Circus came on. Georgie would sit staring at the screen waiting for the cartoons.

Big Top Circus started each week with the face of a clown filling the screen. Georgie was afraid of clowns and he would run from the room screaming. It was almost as entertaining to watch Georgie, as it was to watch the acrobats, trapeze artists and lion tamers on the show.

James hoped that his aunt would have forgotten about the driveway. He knew it was probably too much to hope for, but he could hear that she was on the telephone, and he thought that might give him a reprieve.

"Just a minute, Mildred," he heard Aunt Doris say. "James, there's no television until the driveway is finished."

James dutifully put on his snow pants, coat and galoshes. The mittens that he had worn earlier had dried on the radiator, so at least this time he didn't have to go outside in his mother's pink mitts.

When he got outside, the truck with the plow from Mr. Cooper's car dealership was just finishing their driveway. Mr. Cooper had offered to have it clear the Kelly's driveway too, but James' father had said he's rather James do it to help build his character and stamina for a good day's work.

James thought there were probably a lot warmer ways to build his character.

Light from the Cooper's basement window shone

across the new snow. That meant the Coop was downstairs with his train set, delivering logs to the lumber mill, picking up cans of milk from the farm, and loading up the mail car at the station along his train's route. He'd probably even stage a few horrendous train/cow accidents, using the animals from his toy farm set. If that imaginary farmer couldn't keep his animals off the tracks, then he just had to expect that there would be a few that got maimed or killed when the Cooper 4:15 rolled past the barn.

James knew that Coop's feet had to be a lot warmer than his, even if the socks inside his galoshes were hand-made wool socks that were supposed to keep his toes from falling off.

The snow that was falling now was a lot lighter than the large flakes that had come down earlier in the day. As a result, it made clearing the driveway a lot easier. James thought he might just make it back into the house to see the last few minutes of Big Top Circus.

If only that plow would stay away from Parkland Road.

When the snow was cleared to James' satisfaction, which meant that it was just enough to keep his aunt from sending him back out to do the job properly, he headed for the door. He could see that his aunt was still talking to her friend Mildred on the telephone. She was clearly enjoying herself because she was laughing as hard as James could ever remember seeing, and this was a woman who could laugh at just about anything. She kept daubing at her eyes to stop the tears the laughter was producing from running down her face.

Just as James put his hand on the doorknob, he heard a distant rumble. He thought about what it meant and what his options were. He could wait outside in the cold until the plow made its way down the 700-block of Parkland Road, or he could get creative.

"I'm really tired," he called to his aunt as he headed up the stairs. "I'm going to go to bed."

His aunt was too consumed in her conversation with Mildred to notice that it was the first time James had ever gone to bed without a great deal of prodding. While it was true that he was tired from all of the snow shoveling, he saw it as the perfect way to escape another round with the snow piles left by the plow at the end of the driveway.

He laid in bed, thinking about his father in jail, his mother in the hospital, electric trains, and the overall unfairness of a life that didn't come with x-ray vision. He was asleep before the plow filled in the end of the Kelly's driveway for the third time that day. Had he been awake, he could have seen that the snow was once again falling like giant goose feathers, blanketing the neighborhood, the road, and all of the character and stamina building work he had done clearing the driveway.

Chapter Five

Complications And Calamities

Charles Kelly was not a complicated man. He liked to come home from work, read the newspaper, fall asleep on the couch after dinner, and maybe putter around in his workshop or in his darkroom developing pictures for a while before heading to bed. Not only was he uncomplicated, he didn't like anything to happen that might complicate his life in the least little way.

Ending up in a jail cell on the way home from work was a complication he hadn't counted on ever experiencing.

To make matters worse, he hadn't done anything wrong. Worse still, he had to call his wife's aunt to ask her to help him.

Charles didn't share her sense of whimsy or her ability to laugh at the world. He knew she would find his current predicament to be hilariously funny.

He also knew that she had been just barely able to contain herself when he described what had happened, and he was absolutely certain that she would waste little time before she started sharing the story with her friends.

"She's probably on the phone with Mildred Bidwell right now," he thought as he sat in the holding cell. He tried to reconstruct his day and how it all could have gone so terribly wrong.

The day had started well for him. He had gone home for an early lunch instead of eating at the company cafeteria, because Lorraine had a dentist's appointment in the afternoon. He dropped her off at the dentist's and returned to his office for the afternoon. As he pulled into the parking lot, he saw the first few snowflakes of the season start to drift down from the overcast sky.

Charles knew that Dr. Pappin would probably put her under to pull the wisdom tooth. She would stay under for several hours. Lorraine was the sort of person who could drift into unconsciousness after taking a child's-strength painkiller. She had no tolerance for anesthesia or painkillers. Charles often teased her that she could be out cold after just looking at the bottle the pills came in.

He might have stayed with her, but there had been a memo on his desk that morning directing him to attend a mandatory meeting in the afternoon. Looking back, Charles now wished he hadn't gone back to the office. At two o'clock the entire staff made their way to the meeting on the second floor. No one knew what it would be about, but the most common theory was that it would involve their

Christmas bonuses. When they got upstairs they discovered that some of them had been directed to one room, and the rest to another. Charles was part of the larger group, made up of others in the accounting department, several clerks, and about half of the steno department.

On each chair there was a large manila envelope marked with an employee's name and the words, "Do Not Open Until Directed To Do So."

Eventually, everyone found the chair with their envelope and sat down, now even more convinced that the meeting was about their Christmas bonuses.

A representative from the company's head office stood at the front of the room. When the assembled mass was seated, he read from a prepared statement.

"Ladies and gentlemen, first I would like to thank you all for your many years of service to the company. Your loyalty and service are what makes what I have to say extremely difficult. In order to cut overhead expenses, it has been decided to eliminate the accounting department and hire outside professionals to handle that work in the future. You will each receive a severance package, which is detailed in the envelope you are now holding. Also in that envelope, is a form for you to sign. When you have signed the form, you will be accompanied back to your desk, where you may collect any personal items before leaving the building. Please open your envelopes now."

The room was deathly silent, except for the occasional sniffle by someone trying to avoid tears. Charles opened his envelope. Nearly fifteen years of service was summed up with a check that equated to roughly one month's salary plus his accumulated vacation time giving him another three weeks' pay.

Charles was numb. He stared at the paper for a long time, trying to determine if this was all a dream. Slowly, one by one, staff members brought their signed papers to the front and were escorted out of the room by head office personnel who were waiting for them. The speaker tried to shake hands with them as they dropped off their forms, but most just turned away.

Charles was still staring at the paper, when his boss, Dave Heston, a quiet spectacled accountant, walked slowly up to the front of the room with his form. He set it on the table and turned to the head office representative who offered his hand. Dave looked like he was about to shake hands, but in a quick move brought his fist up under the man's chin and his knee into his groin. The man doubled over in pain, as two of the head office staff grabbed Dave and led him quickly from the room amid a scattering of applause.

Charles finally reached into his pocket for his pen and signed the form. He was then taken in silence back to his desk, where a large box had been placed for his personal items. He packed up his pictures of the family, his coffee mug, and his bowling trophy, and sadly left the building.

The snow had filled the parking lot. He had to brush several inches of it off his car before he could open the doors. He placed the box in the trunk, and sat down behind the wheel. The car struggled to life after several turns of the key. The old windshield wipers fought to keep the glass clear of snow, but it looked like they were in a losing battle. Charles knew he didn't have time to think about what had just occurred. He needed to get to Lorraine, and get them both home before the storm worsened. He hoped that his unexpected early departure from the office would let him beat the traffic, but he could hear cars skidding out on the street.

"Fools must have thought that winter wasn't coming this year. They've waited for the snow to start to put on their snow tires," he said to no one in particular.

Charles didn't condone people who didn't properly prepare for the inevitable. Each year, like clockwork, he would put snow tires on his aging Ford by the twenty-eighth of October. That way he could be sure that he was prepared for the first snowfall, even if it meant driving on snow tires until the middle of December without really needing them.

"Problem with people like that is they turn the road into ice rinks for the rest of us," he continued to himself.

He was right. The drivers who spun their tires on the freshly fallen snow had turned the roads into sheets of ice. During the first few hours of the snowstorm, when the snowflakes had looked like goose feathers it was heavy and wet. As the tires spun, it quickly compressed the fresh snow into ice. As a result, traffic was barely moving.

It took the better part of an hour to go the twelve blocks to Dr. Pappin's office. His prediction about Lorraine's reaction to the anesthesia was right on the mark.

She was still out cold.

Charles and the doctor carried her to the car and

loaded her into the passenger seat. The only indication that she was even alive was the faint moan she gave when they bumped her head on the door of the car.

Charles turned back into the traffic jam that crept along Dundas Street. Lorraine's head pressed against the side window. Her mouth was swollen, and she had a small trickle of dried blood running down her chin, giving her the appearance of a less than victorious boxer after a long fight.

Now that the rest of the workers in the city had gotten out of work, traffic became even more of a problem than it had been on the way to the dentist's office. In the space of half an hour, Charles had only moved three blocks down the street. He could still see the outline of Doctor Pappin's neon tooth sign flashing in his rear-view mirror.

Another half hour passed, and he saw that his gas gauge was getting close to the E. They would never make it home if he didn't stop for gas. He pulled into the first service station he reached.

The attendant came out and started filling the tank. As he did, he looked in through the passenger side window and saw Lorraine.

"This guy must have clocked his wife a good one," thought the attendant. "No one should treat a lady like that."

When Charles inched his way back into traffic, the attendant was on the telephone to the police station.

Charles saw the cruiser's flashing red lights turn on. It was only a block and a half down the street. The siren began to wail and drivers tried their best to give it room to maneuver through the traffic. In the distance, he could hear the wail of an ambulance siren adding to the noise of the car engines and skidding tires.

"Some fool without snow tires probably went and caused an accident," he said, although his wife was not in any condition to hear him.

He turned on the car radio to hear the traffic report that always preceded the 5:45 newscast.

He was surprised to see the police cruiser pull into the gas station parking lot. The officer got out and went into the small office beside the repair bays. In a moment, he reappeared with the attendant, who was pointing at Charles' car.

The officer approached the driver side window. When he knocked on it, Charles jumped in his seat, because he was concentrating on the traffic report.

Charles unrolled his window. Before he could say anything, the officer told him to step out of the car.

"I'm just trying to get back into traffic, Officer," he said, sure that the cop was just going to tell him not to block the sidewalk.

"What did she do to get you so ticked off?" asked the officer.

Charles was confused. "I beg your pardon?"

"The lady there," said the officer motioning towards the unconscious Lorraine. "Did she say something to make you hit her like that?"

"I didn't hit her, she was at the dentist's all afternoon," said Charles, getting a little annoyed with the officer who was delaying his progress towards home.

In a quick move, the officer turned Charles around and put a pair of handcuffs on him. "Try to pull that one over on a judge," he said as he started marching Charles towards the cruiser.

The ambulance pulled into the gas station lot, just as Charles was directed into the back seat of the cruiser. He turned to look at it, and in doing so caused his head to collide with the side of the cruiser. Pain caused him to yell out the words that would have put a bar of soap into James' mouth had he said them.

The officer left Charles in the cruiser and went to help the ambulance attendants load Lorraine onto a stretcher.

"She's really out cold," said one of the attendants. "He must have really walloped her a good one."

While they busied themselves strapping Lorraine onto the stretcher the gas station attendant came out of the office and shouted at Charles, "My old man used to do that to my mother all the time, too. Ain't no way I want to see anyone do that again. I hope they lock you up and throw away the key."

Charles was in shock. He couldn't comprehend what was happening to him. He just wanted to get home, eat his dinner and develop a roll of film in his darkroom before bed. Now, here he was, sitting in the back of a police cruiser like a common criminal, with a lunatic yelling at him through the window.

They left Charles' car at the gas station. There were no available tow trucks to take it to the police impound yard. They were all busy dealing with accidents caused by the storm.

"A wife beater," the cop said to his desk sergeant, as he escorted Charles into the police station. "Knocked his wife out in the car when they were stuck in traffic. She's in emergency at Memorial, completely unresponsive. She doesn't even know what planet she's on. Her face is all swollen and there's blood running out of her mouth."

"Give him his phone call and then put him in the cell until night court convenes, that is if the judge can make it in through the traffic," said the sergeant. "Just what we don't need on a night like this. Some guy who losses it with his wife when were busy enough as it is with all the problems the storm has caused."

"Phone call," thought Charles. "Who do I call?"

He hated the thought of calling Doris with the news that he'd been arrested, especially because somebody thought he had beaten up Lorraine. He didn't want to call Lorraine's brother, because it would take him too long to work out the details of what needed to be done.

"You gonna sit and look at the telephone or are you going to use it?" asked the officer after watching Charles weigh out his options for several minutes.

Charles finally decided that the best option was to swallow his pride and call Mike Cooper, his next-door neighbor. At least Mike had access to the truck with the plow on it and he could get down here a lot faster than anyone else. He dialed Mike's number and listened to it ring.

And ring.

And ring.

The entire Cooper family was out on their front lawn building a snowman that would eventually be standing beside a snow car. The snowman would be given a sign to hold that said, "Even Frosty shops at Cooper Ford!" They did the same thing every year after the first big snowfall.

With no one else to call, he sadly dialed his home number and told the story to Doris. He was tired and more than a little bit annoyed. Hearing Doris trying to stifle her laughter didn't help his mood in the least.

The officer took Charles to a cell that housed several other men awaiting their cases to go to night court, and closed the door behind him. The other men looked scruffy and disheveled. The room had a definite odor that indicated that few if any of his cellmates had seen the wet side of a shower in some time.

Charles sat down to wait for his brother-in-law. He knew it was going to be a while, because John would have to take out his city road map, plot out the best route between his house and the police station and check all the fluid levels in his car before leaving. Traffic would probably still be a nightmare for several hours.

"Damn fool probably hasn't put on his snow tires yet," thought Charles, knowing that John wouldn't waste the energy on such an activity until he absolutely had no other choice. "With my luck, he'll stop on the way here to get it done."

"Whatcha do?" one of the men said.

Charles looked up and saw an old man standing before him. Normally, he would have avoided talking to someone like that, but the man had a kindly face hidden behind a few days growth of beard, and the depression that Charles was feeling needed an outlet. He tried to explain his predicament, even though he didn't really understand how things had gone so wrong because of a simple misunderstanding.

"Well, if you did it, you should be ashamed," the old man said, "and if you didn't I hope you really appreciate the family you have, because no one else in here has anything like that to go home to. Remember, this is the most joyous season."

Charles wasn't in the mood to feel appreciative about anything at that moment. He'd lost his job, gotten arrested, faced a large dentist's bill, and now this old coot wanted him to feel appreciative. It just wasn't going to happen; not after a day like that.

"Most joyous season my ass," he thought.

Eventually a young cop opened the cell door and distributed small boxes to each of the men. It contained a peanut butter sandwich, a can of soda, and a cup of canned peaches.

The other men tore into their sandwiches. Charles looked at his box and sighed. He hated canned peaches. They seemed to epitomize the way the latter part of the day had gone for him. He slowly ate the sandwich, and passed the cup of peaches to the old man who had spoken to him.

Lorraine lay on a stretcher in the emergency ward at Memorial Hospital. She was completely oblivious to her surroundings. She was left alone by the nurses and doctors who were all busy tending to accident victims. They decided the best thing was to let her sleep off the beating she had taken. Had any of them taken a closer look they would have seen the corner of the piece of gauze that Dr. Pappin had put inside her cheek as it slipped between her lips.

Outside, the storm continued. The roads were getting worse, but there were few cars still on the road. Most drivers tried to maneuver safely along the streets. At the top of a hill on Dundas Street, Wayne Darby pulled out of the parking lot at Shamus O'Malley's tavern. He stepped on the gas and raced down the hill. As he neared Valley Drive, the light turned to amber. Again he hit the gas and sailed through the intersection against what was now a red light. A small car had just entered the intersection. Wayne swerved to avoid it and lost control. His car careened along the icy road, vaulted the curb beside a gas station, and smashed into a sedan parked on the lot, pushing it out into the street. The sedan's trunk popped open and a box flew out, depositing a framed family photograph, a stained coffee mug, and a bowling trophy in the snow at the curb.

The gas station was closed. Wayne staggered from his car and looked around. The car he hit was empty and sitting slightly askew at the side of the road. Its driver's side was smashed. One wheel lay in the middle of Dundas Street. Seeing that there had been no witnesses, and realizing that one more drunk driving charge would cost him his license and his job, Wayne jumped back into his own car, and took off.

Steve Murphy crested the hill on Dundas Street a few minutes later. The old plow was rattling and banging along the street, sending arcs of snow cascading along beside it. He looked down the hill and saw a car parked slightly askew in front of the gas station.

Above all else, there was something that Steve could not condone. Everyone knew that as soon as snow started to fall, on-street parking was banned. Still, every snowfall, Steve would see the Plymouth or Chevy belonging to some rich jerk who thought the bylaw didn't apply to him. Steve was determined to teach every one of them a lesson, by adjusting his plow blade to just the right angle that he could completely envelop an illegally parked car with a single pass.

His eyes tightened into a steely glare as he saw Charles' car at the side of the street. It had been a long night, and he wasn't about to let the idiot who had parked on Dundas Street in the middle of the biggest storm in thirty years get away with it. He adjusted the blade, and accelerated down the hill. By the time he crossed Valley Drive, he had a huge pile of snow under the plow, ready to bury the illegally parked sedan. He was so focused on the car, he didn't notice the wheel in the middle of the road. Just as he was about to pull the lever to let the plow release the snow, his left front tire hit the wheel, and caused the plow to jerk to the right. The edge of the blade caught the rear corner of Charles' car and sent it airborne, flipping end over end and back into the gas station parking lot.

Steve quickly checked his mirrors for witnesses,

and seeing none, continued down Dundas Street. As he did, the large back wheel of the plow crushed a framed family photograph.

At almost eleven o'clock, Charles and the others were led into a small courtroom. In his topcoat and suit, he stood out from the mixture of bums and hookers, who all knew that if they pled guilty to whatever they were charged with, they would have to serve fifteen days in the county lock-up. That would put them there for Christmas and the meal the Sisters of Mercy always brought to the prisoners on Christmas Day.

One old hooker, with no teeth in her upper jaw, winked at Charles.

The judge looked tired and frazzled. He barely looked up during the litany of charges being read, prisoners pleading guilty and passing the fifteen-day sentences. It was running with almost assembly line progression.

Until Charles responded, "Not guilty, Your Honor."

The judge was not prepared for this sudden change of pace. He had to look back to see what the person who had disrupted the evening's flow had been charged with. He had long ago stopped listening to the charges and just handed out the fifteen-day sentences that both he and the prisoners wanted.

"Mr. Kelly, it says here that you have been charged with assault causing bodily harm to your wife, one Lorraine Kelly, as you drove along Dundas Street this evening. Your wife is currently a patient at Memorial Hospital being treated for her injuries and was found with her face swollen and bloodied, unconscious in your car with you at the wheel. Are you sure you want to plead not guilty, Mr. Kelly? It seems like an open and shut case against you."

"If I can just explain, Your Honor," started Charles.

"Oh, what the hell," said the judge. "This might be a good one."

"Your Honor," said a visibly nervous Charles, who avoided public speaking at all costs, "I did not assault my wife. I simply picked her up at the dentist's office. She had her wisdom tooth taken out this afternoon and Doctor Pappin put her under to do it. The woman could fall asleep after taking a throat lozenge. She'll be asleep for hours after anesthesia. I tried to tell the officer, but he wouldn't listen to me."

"Pappin?" said the judge. "She was at Painless Pappin's office? I know him. We'll take a ten minute recess while I call him and try to verify what you've said."

When the judge returned to the courtroom a few minutes later it was clear that he had been laughing. His face was red and he had a broad grin.

"Well, Mr. Kelly," he said. "This certainly is one for the books. Painless confirmed your story. Apparently, your wife has quite a reputation in his office. He uses fewer anesthetics on her than he does on a five-year-old. He claims that he once put her under for over an hour by just showing her the needle. I suppose the city and the county owe you an apology. The officer here will drive you back to your car."

Charles was silent through the drive back to the gas station. In the six hours that he had been incarcerated, the snow had built up considerably. The traffic had dissipated and the streets were almost deserted. The fresh snow absorbed much of the sound of the city, making it as quiet outside the car as it was inside.

As they neared the gas station, the officer cleared his throat. "Listen Buddy," he said, "No hard feelings, eh? I was just doing my job."

Charles thought about saying something along the lines of "That's what those generals said at the Nuremburg trials," but he responded with a simple grunt.

Charles often spoke in grunts. Lorraine and the children knew the meaning of most of his grunts. Usually it was just his way of making everyone think he was paying attention to what they were saying.

When the cruiser pulled into the gas station parking lot beside what was left of Charles car, the officer let out a long low whistle. Charles got out of the car and looked at the totally destroyed sedan he had been so unceremoniously hauled out of a few hours before. Back then it was an old car, but a reliable one. Now it was little more than a pile of twisted and dented metal.

"This really isn't your night, is it, Buddy?" said the cop.

Charles couldn't answer him. It all seemed so

totally unreal to him. He walked toward the curb. Something shiny in the snow reflected the light from the streetlights. Charles bent over and picked up the small gold plated statue that had once adorned his bowling trophy. A couple of feet away he found the handle of his coffee mug. He picked up the remnants of a picture frame and pulled the snow crusted photograph of his family from it.

Had it been happening to someone else, Charles might have been able to laugh, but he let loose with a repetitive string of curses that would have made the toothless old hooker from the courtroom blush.

"Calm down, buddy," said the cop, still trying to stifle the laugh that was just barely below the surface. "I'll drive you to the hospital to pick up your wife, and then take you both home. I guess it's the least I can do, eh?"

Charles just nodded.

Lorraine was still sound asleep on the stretcher when they arrived at the hospital. The officer explained the situation to the duty nurse, while Charles looked for a restroom. He heard them both laughing, and knew full well that he was the source of their mirth. When he emerged from the restroom, the officer and the nurse tried to hide their laughter, but were far from successful.

The nurse led them to Lorraine's stretcher. They wheeled it out to the cruiser and managed to get Lorraine into the back seat. It was not a silent trip home. When Lorraine snored, it sounded like a conversation between a wounded elk and a gray whale. Even if they wanted to, Charles and the officer could not have carried out a conversation beneath the din.

Together, they managed to carry Lorraine into the house and upstairs to the master bedroom. Doris put a blanket over her and they all went back downstairs.

When the officer was gone, Charles said, "Thanks for sending someone down there to help me, Doris."

"I did," she said. "I called John as soon as I hung up the phone from you."

Somewhere, out in the night, John Fellows lit a candle from his emergency supply, and covered himself with a blanket. He wondered how long he would have to wait for a tow truck to pull his car out of the snowy ditch. He couldn't understand how he had neglected to consider the possibility of needing his snow tires installed before setting out to rescue his brother-in-law.

Steve Murphy could see John's car from three blocks away when he turned the corner onto Millpond Road. It looked like any of the other illegally parked cars he had buried that night, even if it did seem to be angled a bit toward the ditches that still edged this mostly rural side street on the outskirts of the city. He wondered what the rich jerk who had parked on Dundas Street would think when he returned to get his car. Anyone else might have felt a bit guilty about what he had done to that car, but Steve Murphy was not anybody else.

He was too busy adjusting the angle of his plow

blade to notice the arm waving from the driver's side window of the parked car. He felt the extra snow building beneath him as he prepared to teach another rich jerk a lesson.

John was relieved when he saw the flashing blue light on top of the plow as it rounded the corner three blocks down. He was thankful that he thought to keep a small patch of his side window clear by warming it with the car's cigarette lighter. That way he was able to watch the light grow larger in his rearview mirror. He pulled his blanket tighter around him as he unrolled the window and started waving trying to get the driver's attention. His candle had burned out nearly an hour before, and there hadn't been a single vehicle on the road since.

His hopes lifted as he heard the plow slow down slightly as it approached. The driver must have seen him waving.

Steve slowed down slightly as he neared the illegally parked car. It was a precise move that he'd made a hundred times before. It ensured that he would lay down the greatest load of snow right where he wanted it - directly on top of the rich jerk's car.

As the plow neared John's wave changed from tentative to frantic. He was not used to doing anything fast, but he sensed that he needed to wave with all his might, because the plow driver clearly hadn't seen him. When it was five feet from the back of his car, John realized that he should have used some of his energy to close the car window.

Great clods of snow rained down on the roof of John's old Mercury. As the arc of the snow reached the driver's side window, John was pushed across the front seat by a wall of snow. He felt himself being crushed against the passenger door.

He thought he was about to die. In fact, when he felt himself drift up and out of the car, he was certain that he had died. That was the only explanation he could imagine for the sensation of flying out the door.

He wasn't dead, of course, just flying on a great arc of snow that had filled his car and exploded through the passenger side door taking John with it over the fence on the other side of the ditch. When his velocity could no longer sustain flight, he landed in a heap on the ground.

Pain shot through his body like an electrical shock, probably because that's exactly what it was. One of his boots had been sucked off by the wave of snow and he landed with that foot conveniently resting on an electrified fence. When he finally realized what was happening to him he pulled his leg away from the fence and screamed in agony.

He lay in the snow for several minutes stunned as much by his predicament as by his crash landing. He coughed and sputtered trying to get the snow that seemed to have invaded every orifice in his body.

Inside the plow, that John could see continuing down the road as though nothing had happened, Steve was laughing at the thought of what the rich jerk who parked his car on Millpond Road would think when he returned to it. He didn't realize how short a walk that would be.

John tried to get to his feet. It was clear now that he hadn't died, but thanks to the pain that was building throughout his body, he was beginning to wish he had. After a few attempts, he managed to stand up. His left knee was throbbing, and his right arm hung awkwardly at his side. His coat was filled to capacity with snow and his glasses were gone. The hood of his jacket was also filled with snow, which seemed to have a therapeutic effect on the throbbing head that was jammed in there as well.

He'd been quite proud of himself for preparing for an emergency with his blanket and candle. His pride, or what he had left of it after his unscheduled airborne adventure, slipped away when he looked at the spot where his car was stuck. It seemed to have vanished, but he was sure that it was somewhere under the huge pile of snow. He winced, partially from the pain, and partially from the thought of what the snow would do to the upholstery of the car.

He cursed loudly. It was not something that was normally a part of his vocabulary. He cursed his car, the snow, the snowplow, the snowplow driver, and the pain that continued to shoot through his body. He saved his greatest venom for his brother-in-law, who had been the cause of his need to be driving in that weather in the first place.

He looked down the road. At the next corner, a couple of hundred yards away, someone had erected a Christmas tree lot. He could make out a light coming from the trailer parked on the lot.

Despite the pain, he started to drag his battered body towards the light.

Pat O'Rielly sat in his trailer. With the storm blowing all around him, he knew that there weren't going to be any customers looking for Christmas trees on a night like that. In a way, he was thankful. He was warm and dry inside the trailer, and he had stopped by the liquor store earlier in the day and bought himself an early Christmas gift; a bottle of twelve-year-old single malt scotch.

He sang along with Bing Crosby whose voice crooned out White Christmas from the small portable radio sitting on the counter of trailer beside the still-warm pot full of pork and beans with wieners cut into it. He joined in with Perry Como singing I'll Be Home For Christmas, which never failed to bring a tear to the old Irishman's eye, because like the song said, the only way he'd be home in Dublin for Christmas was "only in me dreams."

It was clear that his self-bought Christmas gift was not likely to last until Christmas. In fact, there was a good chance that the bottle would be drained by the end of that evening's sing-along.

Pat was feeling well into the Christmas spirit. He even did a little jig to the tune of Frosty The Snowman when he got up to serve himself another helping of beans.

That's when John knocked on his door.

Pat continued his jig to the door, wondering what fool would come out on a night like this to buy a Christmas tree. The wind pulled the door handle from his hand and the door flung open against the side of the trailer with a loud bang.

Pat screamed at the sight of a living bruised and

bloodied Frosty the Snowman standing at this door.

John screamed when the pot of beans narrowly missed the side of his head.

When the screaming subsided, Pat realized that what stood before him was a man with snow stuffed in his jacket and all around his head in the hood. His arm hung limp at his side, and he was trying to talk with a couple of broken teeth and a swollen cheek.

Pat helped John up the steps into the tiny trailer and sat him down at the table. He poured a liberal serving of his prized scotch into a glass for John and an even more liberal serving into his own. He downed his, put on his jacket and hurried across the road to the payphone at the gas station on the opposite corner.

Frosty John, the now rapidly melting snowman, stared at the glass. One part of his brain was telling him to drink it to relieve the pain. The other part was replaying the voice of his tea-totaling wife saying, "Lips that touch liquor shall not touch mine."

He decided that he really didn't care if anyone touched his lips again.

As the ambulance driver turned onto Millpond Road, he saw that the plow had already cleared it.

"This guy we're picking up should send a thank you card to the snowplow driver," he said to his partner, "I thought we might not be able to get down Millpond if it hadn't been cleared."

"No one ever appreciates the work done by civil servants like us or that plow jockey," his partner grumbled, "especially on nights like this."

The snow had melted all the way through to his underwear, as John finished off the drink. He could hear the siren in the distance and was thankful that his new friend Pat had called for it. He was also thankful for the bottle of scotch that Pat kept tipping into his glass as he sang along with the Christmas carols on the radio.

Even if he tried especially hard, he couldn't begin to feel thankful for the snowplow driver, though.

Chapter Six

Trying To Find That Joyous Spirit

When James woke up the next morning, he looked into his parent's room. His mother was sound asleep on the bed with a blanket covering her. She was still wearing the same clothes she had been wearing the day before at breakfast.

He looked outside and discovered that his aunt and the weatherman had been right. At least twelve more inches of snow blanketed the ground. It had stopped snowing. The great expanse of fresh snow was difficult to look at. At least the sun was still being filtered through clouds. If the sun hit that snow, it would be blinding.

People up and down the street were shoveling their driveways and sidewalks. James driveway was still full. The plow had deposited another huge pile at the end. There was no sign that his father's car had come in. That worried James.

He quickly dressed for school and ran downstairs to the kitchen. Much to his surprise, his father was sitting at the table, smoking a cigarette and cradling a cup of coffee in his hand. James knew better than to ask him about what had happened the day before. He decided to see if his father would tell him about it on his own.

"So, Aunt Doris says you went Christmas shopping last night. Did you see the train display in the window at Clarkson's?" he said.

"Uhh, yes. Pretty fancy..." replied his father, his voice trailing off, giving the sign that he wasn't really interested in talking.

"Another Christmas lie!" thought James. "Why don't we just put a sign up on the roof that says, 'Santa, don't bother stopping at this house full of liars.'"

"I guess I'd better stay home from school this morning to help you clear the driveway so you can get to work," he said hopefully.

"Don't bother," said his father. "The car isn't here. You can tackle the job when you get home this afternoon."

James ate his breakfast in silence. It was clear that his dad was not in a talkative mood, and James was not feeling all that much like talking either. Something strange was going on, but he didn't really know what it was. He had a sense that yesterday's events would have a lasting impact on his family.

When he had finished his cereal, James said, "My galoshes don't fit over my shoes anymore. I had to shovel the snow last night with just my socks in them."

Charles gave a deep sigh. He was mentally adding up what the previous day had cost him, with the dentist's bill and the hospital bill for Lorraine, needing to replace the car, and now he was going to have to buy new galoshes for James. The severance pay he'd received wouldn't begin to cover it.

"You know," he said, "you'd be a lot taller if you didn't have so much tucked under your legs. Maybe we should just trim your toes so they fit those boots for another year."

James was relieved. As much as it could be annoying having his father comment on the size of his feet, which seemed to be the same size as most of his classmates, it was good to hear his father sounding a bit more like his old self. Whatever had gone on the day before, it didn't take away that continuity that James had grown to count on whenever new shoes or boots were discussed.

"Well," said James, "if I keep shoveling the snow with just socks in my galoshes, my toes might just fall off on their own."

His father smiled at him. It wasn't a big smile. You could tell that he still had a lot on his mind, but it was big enough to reassure James that life would return to normal eventually.

Having broken the ice, James decided that it might be a good time to drop a hint about Christmas, just in case his father really was Santa Claus. He wanted to line all of his ducks up in a row, so he started by trying to elicit some appreciation.

"I shoveled the driveway three times last night. Steve Murphy kept filling in the end of the drive with the plow and the snow didn't seem to let up all evening," he said in a matter of fact tone.

"Thanks son. I owe you one." Charles said more out of habit than out of paying any real attention to what his son was saying.

"Three hundred and twenty eight," said James.

"Huh?" was the only reply Charles had the energy to muster.

"Three hundred and twenty eight. I've been keeping track and you've said 'I owe you one' three hundred and twenty eight times since I started counting."

Charles just smiled a tiny smile and shook his head.

"Sooooo," he said. "Coop is asking Santa Claus for a bunch more cars for his train set. He might even ask for a complete passenger train set to add to the table."

"Mghmph," grunted his father.

James sighed. He might have broken the ice, but it hadn't created a big enough hole to elicit more than a grunt from his dad. He had to hope that Santa had been too busy to hear the Christmas lies coming from 776 Parkland Road. It was probably the only way an electric train would make it into the Kelly house that year.

"There's a note on the fridge that you are supposed to bring a grocery sack to school this morning," said his father. "Better not forget. I don't want your mother to get any more calls from your teacher saying you forgot to bring things."

James was notorious for forgetting to bring things to school, thereby causing his mother to take Georgie out and deliver the items to his classroom.

Charles remained seated at the table while his son finished getting ready for school. Right behind James, his daughter Louise repeated the process and gathered her things.

The children said goodbye and Charles was left alone with his coffee and his thoughts. The previous day had been a hard one for him to swallow. His pride was damaged. He'd lost his job, and someone thought that he had struck his wife, something he would never in his wildest dreams think of doing. He realized he had few friends he could call at his hour of need, and even his own brother-in-law had left him sitting in jail.

Charles was as depressed as he could ever remember being. The loss of his job was a bitter pill. He had been a loyal company man for better than fifteen years, and he expected a little loyalty in return. He hadn't told anyone about what had happened, and he decided that he would try to keep it to himself, at least for the time being. He needed time to think things through.

Doris came into the room with Georgie and lifted the boy into his high chair.

"Lorraine is still asleep," she said. "I guess old

Painless really knocked her for a loop this time."

Charles just grunted a reply, much the same way as he had responded to his son earlier. He was too deep in his thoughts and his funk for small talk.

Somewhere deep in his mind a thought was forming. He heard the old man from the cell say, "I hope you really appreciate the family you have, because no one else in here has anything like that to go home to." Maybe it was time he made some changes. Maybe all of the calamities of the previous day were trying to tell him something. He adored his wife and he had three good kids. Perhaps he had been taking all that for granted a little too long. He even had a couple of friends, but he had never been the most sociable individual in the group. Maybe he was taking his friends for granted too.

It wasn't like Charles to be introspective, but working those thoughts through his mind seemed to make him feel a bit better.

Charles told Doris that he had decided to use up some of his vacation time. He suggested that it was because the holiday season was coming, and he'd like to try to enjoy it without thinking about work, or jail cells. He got up, poured himself another cup of coffee and pretended to call his office to let the boss know he wouldn't be in for a couple of weeks. He explained the events of the night before into the receiver. He knew that Doris was listening and he had to make the call sound realistic, so he stopped every so often to say, "Quit laughing Dave. It isn't funny." He hung up the phone after wishing the dial tone a merry Christmas.

❀ ❀ ❀

James met Coop out on the sidewalk. The two boys would walk to school together on those days when they were best friends, and avoid one another on days when they were mortal enemies. James was glad his friend wasn't angry that he had used the training bra incident to get him to keep quiet about seeing him in pink mittens the night before. As they walked, they talked about Christmas. It was good way to get the other things off James' mind.

"I'm going down to Clarkson's after school today to make a list of all the things I want Santa to bring for my train set this year," said Coop. "Wanna come with me?"

"Can't," said James. "I have to shovel out the driveway after school so Dad can get the car into the garage tonight."

When the boys reached the school, they sat on a bench in the hall outside their classroom taking off their boots. James had carried his shoes to school in a bag. He struggled to pull off his galoshes. Even with just socks inside them, they were still tight. He didn't notice Miss Witherspoon watching.

"Poor child," she said to herself. "His parents can't even afford new galoshes for him."

It wasn't that the Kellys couldn't afford new boots; it just wasn't something that anyone had thought about before he took them out of the closet the previous night.

Miss Witherspoon brought a small pine tree into the classroom that morning, and the children were excited to see it. There were still four days before school got out for the Christmas vacation, and the arrival of the class Christmas tree signaled the start of less work and more fun in the classroom.

After the morning announcements, Miss Witherspoon waited for the children to settle down in their seats. She had a large pile of red and green construction paper in her hands. The children knew the significance of that.

"We will dedicate this entire morning to art class so that we can make decorations for our tree," she announced.

The fourth grade classroom erupted in a loud cheer that could be heard throughout the school.

Each child made an outline of his or her hand on a piece of construction paper and cut out the mitten shapes. Cotton balls were glued onto them to provide trim. The all wrote their names neatly on their paper mitts, so that their parents could pick them up and take them home when they came to the parent teacher meeting just before the holidays began.

"Want me to see if I can get you a piece of pink construction paper to make your mitten," Coop whispered across the aisle to James.

James just looked at Coop and put his hands over his chest signifying the shape of a bra. Coop quickly - and quietly- returned to work on his bright green mitten.

By the time the children were ready to eat their lunches, the classroom had taken on a festive appearance. The colorful mittens hung from the tree boughs. The school janitor, Mr. Roney, known by the students and teachers alike as Mac Roney, came in with his ladder. He strung the great lengths of red and green chains the children had made from loops of construction paper across the tops of the blackboards. It was the best morning James could remember having in Miss Witherspoon's class.

In the afternoon, Miss Witherspoon brought out sheets of white paper. She taught the children to make snowflakes by folding the paper and cutting small pieces from it. When they unfolded the paper, they saw snowflakes that looked like the giant ones that had fallen from the sky the previous day.

They glued the snowflakes to the paper bags they had all brought from home. After writing their names on the bags, they were pinned in alphabetical order to the chalk holder under the blackboard at the front of the room. They would serve as the children's mailboxes for Christmas cards or, in the case of Irv Weinstein and Sadie Bromberg, Hanukkah greetings.

James felt sorry for Irv and Sadie. Santa didn't visit the Jewish kids' houses in the neighborhood, and they didn't have Christmas trees. His mother always made sure he included them in holiday greetings with the most non-Christmassy cards he could find in his package of 50 children's greetings.

She also put a special candlestick in the front window with nine electric candles in it. She said that was to let the Jewish neighbors know that they were always welcome. Every day during Hanukkah, she would light an additional candle, and she sent James to school with an extra cookie to give to Irv and Sadie.

James didn't really understand it, but he chalked it up to Irv's mother being one of Lorraine's best friends.

It was a great day at school. Miss Witherspoon never completely dedicated a whole day to fun activities before. He kept waiting for the other shoe to drop and have her spring a surprise arithmetic quiz or spelling test on them. It never came. By the end of the day, the room was fully decorated for Christmas.

When school ended, James and Coop walked home quickly. Coop was in a hurry so that he could spend as much time as possible at Clarkson's determining which items from the selection of train cars, track and accessories he would put on his letter to Santa Claus. James was in a hurry so that he could create a stockpile of snowballs at the far side of the house for the ambush he had planned for Louise in retaliation for the previous day's unprovoked attack.

Halfway home he remembered the driveway. The great Louise ambush would have to wait for another day. He knew that he had a couple of hours of shoveling ahead of him before his father could get the car into the garage.

People had cleared their driveways and sidewalks all along Parkland Road. They had created piles of snow across their front yards that were taller than James. It was like walking through a snow tunnel. As a result, he couldn't see his own house until he reached his driveway.

When he got there, James stopped. He couldn't

believe his eyes. The driveway was completely cleared. There was even gravel showing through the snow in a few spots.

James entered through the back door of the house so that he wouldn't spread snow in the front hall. His father and Aunt Doris were sitting at the kitchen table drinking coffee. He was surprised to see his father at that hour of the day.

"Hi Dad," James said. "The driveway looks great. It must have taken a long time to shovel that much snow."

Charles Kelly smiled at his son. "No, it only took a few minutes, James. You just have to know the right way to do it."

He knew the right way to clear the driveway, all right. When he looked at the snow, and heard from Doris about how many times James had already cleared it, He called Mike Cooper, down at his car dealership, and asked if he could get the driveway cleared by Mike's driver when he came to finish of theirs.

"Anytime," said Mike. "Say isn't it about time you got rid of that old Ford you're toting your family around in. I have a new station wagon down here at the lot that I could let you have for a great price. You know me, Charlie-boy, I practically give cars away."

Charles bristled at being called Charlie-boy, and Mike knew it, but they had been neighbors for more than ten years, and he'd called him that ever since the day they met.

They were good neighbors, too. They each watched the other's house when one would take a vacation. Charles always bought enough fertilizer to do both yards. He would say he did it to make sure that weeds didn't take root in Mike's lawn and spread into his. Mike cut both front yards because he said he didn't want old Charlie to have a heart attack out front where everyone on the street could see him. They even kept a few bottles of the other's favorite beer in their refrigerators on hot summer days, so that they would have someone to sit outside with, listening to a ballgame on the radio.

"I might have to ask Santa Claus about a new car, Mike," Charles said. "Mine is going to be towed down to your lot later today."

That got Mike's interest. He knew that Charles wasn't the sort of man to talk trade until he absolutely had to do it. He wondered what had happened to bring about the change. In his wildest dreams he couldn't have imagined.

Charles knew that eventually, he'd have to tell Mike the whole story about the previous night, so he might as well get it over with.

"Okay, Mike, I'll tell you about it, but you have to promise not to laugh," said Charles, knowing full well that even if Mike did promise it was going to be impossible for him to stick to his word.

Charles didn't talk about what had gone on in the office, just the events surrounding Lorraine's visit to the dentist, and his trip to jail. Several times through the story, Mike begged Charles to stop and let him catch his breath. He hadn't laughed that hard in a long, long time. His sides hurt and his staff kept looking in through his office door to see if he had lost his mind.

"I'll send the truck over to take care of your driveway and then he can go and pick up your car and tow it in. We'll get you fixed up, but you really should have a look at these wagons. One of them is sure to have your name on it," said Mike, ever the salesman.

Mike set the telephone receiver down and laughed until he was red in the face. A couple of times he started to tell his secretary what he was laughing about, but could only get a couple of words out before the picture of Charles sitting in a jail cell came back into his mind and he would lose control of his laughter again.

Charles' face was also red. It was embarrassing to have to tell Mike what had happened to him. He was also worried about his employment situation, and how he would pay for a replacement vehicle.

James sat down in front of the plate of cookies and the glass of milk Doris had put by his place. He forgot about the plan to retaliate against his sister for the snowball attack of the day before.

"Can I go with Coop down to Clarkson's to look at the electric trains?" he asked. "Coop is going to make a list of the things that he's going to ask Santa Claus to bring him."

"Go catch him before he leaves and I'll walk

down there with you. I have to go see Mr. Cooper,"
said Charles. "While we're there I guess we'd better
get you some new galoshes. They could be your
Christmas present."

James searched his father's face looking for a sign
that he might be kidding. He was pretty sure he
found it in the upturned corners of the man's mouth,
but he wasn't positive. The thought gnawed at him.
It was just the sort of thing he might have expected to
find under the tree; that and the warm socks to keep
his toes from falling off.

Together, Coop, James and his father walked
along through the piles of snow toward Clarkson's
Department Store. The boys knew that of all the
department stores in town, Clarkson's was the place
where Santa shopped for the things the elves
couldn't make for him. They were pretty sure that
the Santa Claus who sat in a giant throne at the edge
of the toy department at Clarkson's was the real one,
not the people you saw dressed like Santa at other
stores or on the street corners ringing bells.

The Kellys were quiet as they walked along. It
wasn't so much by choice as because Coop kept a
steady stream of words flowing from his mouth. He
had already gotten a good idea about what pieces of
train gear he wanted and he was telling the James
and his father about each and every one of them.

James wondered if Santa Claus could fit all that
in his sleigh and still have room for gifts for other
children. He especially hoped that Christmas
morning would bring him more than just warm
socks, galoshes and a couple small items. He'd really
worked hard at being good this year.

❀ ❀ ❀

Charles wandered into the hubbub of the toy department at Clarkson's along with the two boys. Normally he would have avoided the place like the plague, but Coops enthusiasm for the trains had gotten to his curiosity. He could scarcely believe his eyes when he saw the train display that took up a huge section of floor space, in what was the garden furniture department at other times of the year.

With all the snow outside, it was unlikely that anyone would be thinking about folding chaise lounges at this time of year, so Clarkson's packed all of that stock in their warehouse, and made room for what had become the holiday season's most impressive display, and biggest purchase lure for fathers who could be dragged in by their sons.

Charles couldn't remember ever going into the toy department of Clarkson's. When he was a boy, he knew that there was little chance his mother would ever spend any money on something as frivolous as a toy, so there was little point of ever looking at them. Since the children arrived, the job of buying Christmas presents and birthday gifts had always fallen to Lorraine. She liked shopping for clothes, so she also rarely set foot in the overcrowded Toyland. The toys that arrived under the Kelly Christmas tree were usually small die-cast cars and trucks for the boys that she could pick up at Stigman's grocery store when she did her weekly shopping and handmade dolls for Louise that came from the church's Christmas bazaar .

Charles stood transfixed watching a miniature locomotive train pulling a dozen different cars along the track heading toward a trestle bridge over a mountain ravine. A passenger train, complete with a dining car, a modern aerodynamic locomotive, and several passenger cars with viewing domes mounted on their tops, followed the locomotive along the track adjacent to the freight train. Inside the clear domes, Charles could see tiny passengers, sitting, looking back out the windows toward him.

In another section of the display, there was a miniature freight yard, built with rows of track, and engines shunting cars back and forth into position. There were cars carrying miniature automobiles, including several of those new station wagons that Coop's father had been talking about. Another row of track held train cars piled high with logs, waiting their turn at the miniature mill. As the engine brought the log tenders up to the mill, they would dump their load by lifting one side of the car, until the logs tumbled out.

At the center of it all was a train station with its own, equally busy set of tracks. A passenger train, just like the one that was now rolling through the mountain pass that opened up at the end of the trestle, sat beside the station's platform. Two dozen miniature people stood along the platform, seemingly waiting to board, or watching for miniature relatives to disembark from the train.

At another platform across the tracks from the station, a small freight train stood waiting. Behind its engine and coal car, there was a mail car and a refrigerated car. Miniature cans of milk lined the platform beside the refrigerator car, and tiny bags of mail, and wagons filled with parcels stood beside the mail car, waiting to be loaded.

Without warning the passenger train at the station blew its whistle, and started heading down the tracks. It switched from the siding onto a main line of track and headed off around a bend and into a tunnel. As the last car entered the tunnel, another whistle blew. The passenger train that had been at the far end of the display earlier rounded a curve and entered the station from the other end, pulling up behind the station and stopping. A moment later, the train that left the station emerged from the tunnel and headed for the trestle where Charles had first seen the now stationary train.

He could barely believe his eyes. He had no idea that the simple trains he had known as a child, could have developed into such a wondrous sight. He barely even noticed Coop standing beside him, giving a running play-by-play of everything that was going on. The boy could identify every single piece of equipment that was in use on the display, explain how it worked, and what it would cost should Santa not be able to deliver it on Christmas Eve.

James just stood watching everything. He knew that the chances of ever seeing any of it under his Christmas tree were remote at best. If he was lucky there might be a couple of small toys in with the traditional socks and underwear that he'd be unwrapping, and forced to sound grateful for, even though it was very hard to come up with something that sounded like gratitude when faced with a three-pack of tidy-whities.

Charles looked around the display. There was a scattering of other fathers, all seeming to be equally amazed at the sights and sounds from the train display. Two dozen other boys were watching the trains. Some of them were dutifully filling out lists in notebooks, in preparation for their letters to Santa.

Off to the side, watching the fathers, was one of Clarkson's salesmen. He knew that once a father had a chance to watch the trains in the display, there was a very good chance that they would be back later to make a purchase. He paid particular attention to Charles. It wasn't often that you saw a father so completely mesmerized by what he was watching. If ever he saw a sale waiting to happen, it was Charles. He just wasn't sure how much money he'd able to talk him into spending.

Before he could make his way through the crowd to talk to Charles, he found his way blocked by a kid with a large notebook filled with lists of train accessories. Coop was determined to bend the salesman's ear about all of the products featured on the display.

The salesman tried to sidestep Coop, who he recognized from previous lengthy discussions about all things related to the trains, but Coop deftly matched him step for step.

Sadly, he watched Charles Kelly look at his watch, a sure sign that he was about to leave. He knew that there was no way he could make it past Coop and across the floor past a dozen other kids just like him before Charles headed for the door.

"He'll be back," he thought. "I've seen that look a hundred times before. He wants the train as much as his kid does."

❀ ❀ ❀

Charles was oblivious to the salesman's gaze. He had seen the price tag on one of the smaller train sets, and couldn't imagine spending that much money on a toy, especially with no job to return to after Christmas. He looked at his watch and realized that he didn't have much time before Cooper Ford would be closing for the day.

He leaned down and said to James, "I've got to get going. You and Coop should head for home. I'll see you there when I get back from picking up the car."

James watched his father head for the door of Clarkson's Department Store. He had desperately wanted to drop a few hints about the train sets, just in case his father had Santa's ear, or if the older kids were right and he was Santa.

He would have been happy with the most basic set, a bit of track, a locomotive, and a couple of cars, but he could see his opportunity to let his father know about that slipping away as Charles pushed his way into the revolving door at the front of the store.

It was going to be a long walk home listening to Coop talk about all the new products that the store had added to the display. Coop was sure, and justifiably so, that many of them would be found under his tree on Christmas morning.

James pictured warm woolen socks and white

underwear, along with the new pair of galoshes that his father had forgotten to buy.

Chapter Seven

It's A Gift The Whole Family Can Enjoy

Charles had a lot to think about as he walked from Clarkson's to Cooper Ford. He was a man who liked to be sure about everything, and the last twenty-four hours had shaken him greatly. He had been sure he would never see the inside of a jail cell, but he had become all too familiar with the sights and especially the smells of a holding cell on the previous night. He had also been sure that he would never be unemployed. A bookkeeper may not have been the most exciting career in the world, or the best paying, but he always thought it was something that would pay the bills and keep him employed until he was old enough to retire. That whole combined experience of the previous day had shaken him and his outlook on how life was supposed to unfold.

He had to admit to himself that he was not all that sure about what being a father was all about, despite having been in that role for over ten years. His own father had died when he was just five years old. It left him as the only son of an embittered woman unhappy in her role of raising a child alone. As a result, Charles did not have the slightest idea about the desires of a young boy because he had not been allowed to express them when he was growing up.

Watching those electric trains at Clarkson's had somehow tapped into those deeply repressed feelings of being a kid wanting nothing more than the enjoyment that a toy like that could bring.

He had absolutely no idea what to do with or about those feelings, and before he could think about it any further he discovered that he had already reached the parking lot of Cooper Ford.

He could see Mike Cooper was talking on the phone inside the dealership. Mike was laughing uproariously. Charles had a sense that he, and the events that had befallen him the night before might have been the topic of conversation.

He waved to Mike and walked around the lot. He didn't want to go inside just in case he heard Mike telling - and embellishing - the story. He stopped and looked at a couple of second-hand cars at the far end of the lot. He hoped there might be something there that he could afford. The cold air started to cut through to his bones, and he decided to head inside to wait for Mike. As he got close to the building, he saw the station wagon, parked in front of the doors so that anyone who wanted to enter the building would have to take a good look at it on the way past.

It was a thing of beauty, unlike the frumpy old sedans Charles had always driven. The sides of the car were polished wood. The rest of the body was waxed to a glistening sheen. Inside there were three rows of seats; room for the whole Kelly family and Aunt Doris to boot. The sign in the car's side window said it came with an automatic transmission - no more shifting on the long drives in heavy traffic.

Charles circled the car the way James and Coop had circled the train display at Clarkson's. He took in every detail about the car's exterior and interior. It was called the Squire. He was already picturing himself behind the wheel with his family loaded in for a drive in the country. Lorraine was by his side in the passenger seat. James, Louise and Georgie sat together in the second row, and Doris was in the very back. That last image made him smile broadly because the back seat faced toward the rear of the car, so Doris would be riding backwards and unable to comment on his driving.

He shook his head to bring himself back from the reverie. Clearly a car like that was not even remotely in his budget right now. He was right. When he made his way to the front of the car, he spotted the price sticker. Two thousand, four hundred and fifty dollars. That was over half of a year's take-home pay when he had a pay to take home. The image of the Kelly family riding down the highway in the Squire started to evaporate.

❀ ❀ ❀

Mike Cooper hadn't really been talking to anyone on the phone. He had seen Charles walking up the street toward the dealership and he decided to use the little ruse to give Charles an opportunity to take a good look at the Squire. He parked the car in such a way that Charles couldn't miss it, and he stood, telephone receiver to his ear, watching Charles look at the car. When he saw the expression on his face turn to dismay at the sight of the price sticker, he knew it was time to go out and talk to his neighbor.

"Isn't she a great piece of American workmanship, Charlie-Boy," he said as he came through the door.

"Mghmph," Charles replied, already giving up on the idea of making Doris face the back of the car on their family outings.

"Your assessment of the damage to your old sedan was right, Charlie-boy. It is totaled. I hope you had it insured," Mike said, hoping that with the insurance money, and whatever Charles could part with on his own, he might just sell him on the idea of the Squire.

I doubt if the insurance will give me much for the old one, Mike," Charles said, looking at the floor instead of at his neighbor. "I think I'm going to have to consider one of the ones you have down in the used car lot."

"Of course, I could always send you home in the

Squire here…"

"Right," said Charles. "I'm not a rich car dealer like you. I could never afford that price for a car."

Actually, Charles could afford it, thanks to a couple of aunts who felt sorry for him for being raised by his mother. They had taken good care of him in their wills. The house on Parkland Road was the bequest of one aunt. A nice nest egg in government bonds came from another. Charles just didn't want to part with any of it if he could avoid it.

Still, he really did like that car and he did plan to make some changes in his life, didn't he?

"Charlie-Boy, you don't think that price sticker is what you'd have to pay, now do you? I'm sure I could knock a dollar or maybe two off that for a neighbor,"" Mike said with a wink.

Charles looked out the window and saw his old crumpled sedan parked in the back corner of the lot waiting for the scrap dealer to pick it up. It seemed to be the polar opposite of the shiny new Ford Squire the two men were leaning against in the late afternoon winter sun.

"Come on into the office, Charlie-Boy. I have a bottle of scotch in there calling our names. It's too cold out here to talk."

The two men walked into Mike's office. He pulled out an unopened twenty-six-ounce bottle of very well aged scotch, and poured each of them a healthy serving.

"A gift from one of our suppliers," Mike said nodding at the bottle.

The two men sat and savored the warmth of the scotch as it slid down their throats. Neither of them spoke for several minutes. Mike refilled the glasses, and Charles felt warm and relaxed; just the way Mike hoped he'd feel.

"So, about that Squire…"

Charles held his hand up like a traffic cop signaling a stop.

"Mike," he said, "I really do like that wagon, but it is just too expensive, even if you do knock a dollar or two off the price."

"Give me a minute to write it down, because this scotch seems to be erasing my ability to do arithmetic in my head. I'll take the price I actually need to sell the car for, minus what I can get for yours, plus the cost of getting your driveway plowed out today… just kidding Charlie-boy, just kidding."

Mike pondered the numbers he had written down on the page for a long time. He took a few gulps of the scotch and refilled both their glasses.

"OK," he said, "I'll send you home in the Squire right now, with a full tank of gas, snow tires, and I'll take whatever you get from your insurance company and the cash we'll get from the scrap dealer for your old one, as a down payment. You come back after New Year's with a check for this amount."

He handed Charles the slip of paper. Charles looked at it, and then at his glass. It was obvious the scotch was playing tricks with his eyes, because the number was far lower than he could have ever imagined.

He knew he was feeling the same way about the car as James and Coop felt about those toy trains. He really wanted it.

"I don't know what to say, Mike," he said, "That's an incredibly generous offer, but I just can't swing it right now."

"Look Charles," said Mike, sounding serious for the first time in the ten years Charles had known him. "Our wives are best friends. Our boys are best friends and sometimes mortal enemies. You and I have helped each other out ever since we first met. If I go home and tell Jeanie that I didn't help you out with this car mess you've gotten yourself into, I might as well pitch a tent in the snow in the back yard. Take the car as a courtesy car while we wait for you to come to your senses. You need something to drive for the next couple of weeks, and I'll let you use the Squire for now."

The two men shook hands. For a moment Charles felt like hugging Mike, but that would have crossed a line that neither one of them would have been comfortable with.

"Here are the keys Charlie-boy. Go out and read the first few pages of the owner's manual before you start her up. It's in the glove compartment. I'll clean up here and you can give me a ride home in your new car."

Charles could scarcely believe what had just happened to him. He felt the way he had so often wished he could feel as a kid, but he knew that his mother would not have approved of kid-like behavior. The new Ford Squire released the kid in him like a genie escaping form a bottle. He couldn't wait to see Lorraine's face when she saw it.

He just didn't know how he was going to pay for it with no paycheck coming in anymore. He could have taken the money out of his savings, but the fear of living without a big nest egg to fall back on in hard times was almost overpowering.

In fact, he couldn't wait to see his own face. He walked up to the driver's side door and bent down to look in the rear-view mirror. The face that looked back at him reminded him of someone, but it wasn't the normal reflection he saw in mirrors. This face suddenly understood that sometimes a material object could bring happiness, or something closely resembling it, to one's life.

"Money can't buy happiness," he thought, "but I'm going to be able to park this new Ford Squire next to it."

Charles dropped Mike off at the end of his driveway and slowly pulled into his own next door.

Lorraine heard the car in the driveway, but she knew immediately it wasn't Charles in the old sedan. The car was simply not making enough noise. She looked out the side door in time to see Charles emerge from the driver's seat of the Ford Squire.

She was surprised, but only partially by the sight of the new car. What really took her aback was the look on Charles' face. He was actually laughing.

"Have you been drinking?" she asked.

"Just a little," laughed Charles. "How do you like the car?"

Lorraine wasn't sure what to say. Finally, she asked where the sedan was. Charles told her the story about what had happened the night before. She had been there, but was unconscious through the entire event, so it was all news to her. Several times during the retelling of the events (with the exception of the job situation that Charles hadn't figured out how to break to her yet) she gasped and held her hand to her mouth.

"So the old car is a wreck. Mike leant me this one while we try to decide what to do about replacing it. This sure is a nice car, and he's offered me an incredible price for it, but I just don't know if we can afford it right now." Charles continued. "We'll have to sleep on it for a day or two."

The children heard the commotion in the driveway and pressed their faces against the side window.

Georgie kept repeating, "New car! New car!"

Louise asked James if there would be room for a pony in the new car. It seemed everything in her life these days rotated around her illogical wish to have a pony residing in their back yard.

James realized what the car meant. It meant that a lot of money had just been spent, and with barely a week to go before Christmas, it was unlikely that there would be much under the tree. He had heard before that some major expense was a gift for the whole family and he expected that the new car would fit nicely into that category. Two years before the whole family were supposed to be thrilled with new living room furniture, but it was hard for James to get too excited about something he was only allowed to sit on if there was a towel or a blanket between him and the upholstery.

He returned to his room and flopped on the bed.

"If Dad really is Santa, he just spent all the money on a new sleigh," he thought.

Charles saw his son's face before he turned and left. He knew what he was thinking. Once again he heard the old man say, ""I hope you really appreciate the family you have, because no one else in here has anything like that to go home to."

Aunt Doris called the children to supper. James listened to his sister and brother scamper down the stairs to the dining room. He didn't feel much like eating, but he knew that if he didn't he'd be hearing the story about the starving children in Africa or China or some other faraway place.

When he arrived, the rest of the family was already sitting at the table.

"Nice of you to join us, James," Charles said.

James was quiet through the meal, not that he had a lot of choice. Louise had gotten a hold of the Clarkson's Christmas catalog that afternoon and had spent most of the time reviewing the list of things she would like Santa to bring her this Christmas. Charles wasn't sure, but he had a pretty good idea that her list included everything on pages eighteen through twenty-four inclusive, plus the top half of the back cover.

Those were the pages, James avoided. They involved image after image of dolls, dollhouses, doll clothes, and doll accessories.

Louise was able to recite the contents of those pages with incredible accuracy. As a result, she monopolized the dinner conversation. Even if James had felt like talking, he couldn't have gotten a word in edgewise.

And James did not feel like talking.

He had seen the commercials on television for new cars. He knew that they cost more money than he could ever imagine seeing in one place, and yet somehow, his father had gone out and brought home a new car that afternoon, without even telling anyone he was going to do it.

If a new car had been in the cards for the Kelly family, James would have heard about it sitting at the listening post at the top of the stairs.

"Stupid girl," thought James. "She doesn't have a clue that this year we'll get some socks and underwear, and you can bet that there will be an announcement that the car is a gift for the whole family."

There was something odd about his father. Throughout the entire meal, he had sat at his place at the end of the table and actually seemed like he was listening to Louise prattle on about the new Barbie and Ken dolls, their imaginary friends, clothes and accessories.

Even stranger, he hadn't once told Doris that the meat could have been used to repair his old shoes. Charles enjoyed comparing his aunt-in-law's cooking to leather tanning.

Lorraine didn't do much talking either. Dinner

for her consisted of a bowl of soup because she was just not ready to try chewing again after the dentist had tortured her mouth the day before. She was still trying to remember whether briefly waking up in a hospital room was a dream of if it had actually happened. According to the story Charles had just related to her, it was all too real.

She had read an article in a magazine that said that sometimes people say things under anesthesia that they wouldn't normally say when conscious. She blushed at the thought of what she might have said.

Georgie sat in his highchair beside his mother. He also had a special meal so that he wouldn't have to try to chew Doris's roast beef. Occasionally he'd blow bubbles in his milk in an effort to attract some attention away from Louise's litany of doll paraphernalia.

It didn't work.

Dessert was one of Doris' specialties: a concoction that resembled pudding that failed to set. It was sickeningly sweet and no one could identify what it was supposed to be. When Doris was outside of hearing range, James referred to it as cream of pudding soup.

When dinner ended, Doris cleared the table while Lorraine took Georgie upstairs for his bath. Louise headed back into the living room to reexamine the Clarkson's catalog in case there was something she had missed in her previous perusal.

Charles lit a cigarette and poured himself another cup of coffee from the percolator on the counter. James was about to excuse himself when his father cleared his throat. The sound startled James, because his father so rarely said anything at the table.

"So," said Charles, "those trains were really something down at Clarkson's this afternoon."

"Uh-huh," replied James, not wanting to show his excitement for the topic.

"I remember my toy train," continued Charles. "It had a round track and a wind-up locomotive with three cars. My Aunt Anne brought it over one Christmas. My mother wasn't too impressed."

"You had a train set?" James could hardly believe it. There just might be hope for another year when Christmas wouldn't include a new car as a gift for the whole family.

"Well, it sure wasn't anything like what we saw today, but it kept me a lot more entertained than the copy of The Iliad my mother gave me that year."

"Waste of money," muttered Doris, who had come back into the dining room to see if Charles had finished with his coffee cup. "Toys don't keep your feet warm."

James didn't get a chance to press his father for more details about what he had thought about the train display at Clarkson's before the doorbell rang and the door flung open.

Everyone in the house knew what that meant. The only people who ever rang the doorbell and then walked right in were Uncle John and Aunt Millicent.

James had often heard his mother mutter, "That woman! She thinks if she rings the bell it's her right to waltz right in whether she's welcome or not."

It was unlikely that Millicent was welcome in too many places. Opinionated, bigoted, and as Charles would say, "without the brains God gave a gnat," Millicent Brooks was an imposing woman.

She imposed herself on everyone she knew.

John was a sight to behold. His left arm was in a cast. He had bandages on several places on his face and hands and he was walking with one crutch propped under his arm.

Charles knew that whatever the story was, it was going to take a long time for John to tell it. James took his opportunity and ran for the stairs, saying he had forgotten some homework. His father watched him climb the stairs wishing that he could have an excuse to go to his room and avoid an evening with John and Millicent.

"John could have gotten himself killed last night trying to get you out of jail," Millicent said pointing a finger at Charles. "And what thanks does he get? No one so much as picked up the phone to see if he was OK."

Doris and Lorraine exchanged glances. Neither of them wanted to look at Millicent. It wasn't because they were feeling particularly guilty about the topic of her rant. They were more afraid that if they looked at her they would start laughing.

James looked at the calendar on his bedroom wall. Christmas was still seven days away, but more importantly the last day of school before the holidays was the following Tuesday. This was one of the years that gave the students their longest Christmas break. The holiday fell on Thursday, so they would be off until the Monday after New Year's.

That thought filled him with a sense of relief and dread. Grade four was a lot harder than grade three had been. The first day of school seemed like it had been a lot further back than just over three months. He was really looking forward to twelve days without getting up for school, without dealing with Miss Witherspoon, and, even better, having the pinnacle day of the year thrown into the middle of it. On the other hand, he also knew that between now and December twenty-third he would have to write tests in every subject.

In reality, James was a pretty good student. He did well in arithmetic. He enjoyed learning about the battles in history, and he could name all fifty states and all ten Canadian provinces. Still the prospect of tests made him nervous.

When he finished his homework, he had a decision to make. TV was out for the night thanks to the arrival of Uncle John and Aunt Millicent. Aunt Millicent didn't believe in owning a television and felt that they were a sure sign that the devil was alive, well and working to bring down society as she would have it. In order to avoid hearing her lecture on the subject the Kelly children had learned to avoid turning on the television when she was in the house.

If he went downstairs, he would have to sit with the adults and listen to his aunt prattle on about whatever was on her mind. He'd love to go out and fool around in the snow, but he would never make it past the living room without being called to sit with his relatives.

He was trapped.

He walked over to the calendar on his wall. The

picture for December was a scene of kids playing hockey on a backyard skating rink while Christmas lights shone around the houses in the background. He wished something like that could be in his backyard, but he had learned over the years that it would not get past his father's desire for the perfect lawn.

He carefully crossed December eighteenth off with his red pen by drawing a neat X through the date. Only seven days to go.

He sat on his bed with a comic book, generally feeling sorry for himself. He thought about just how unfair his life was. He was facing the prospect of Christmas that he knew would be largely centered on gifts that were practical not fun. He couldn't skate in his backyard. He couldn't go into his basement and play with an electric train set. Everything that he wanted seemed to be next door and in the possession of his best friend and sometimes mortal enemy, Coop.

James heard his father coming up the stairs. He went into the bathroom and spent several minutes in silence. James knew that his father was rarely silent in the bathroom, so he knew the trip was just an excuse for his father to get a break from his in-laws.

Eventually the toilet flushed, causing pipes to rattle throughout the old house. His father came out of the bathroom, but rather than heading for the stairs he slipped into James' bedroom and closed the door.

"Just go along with me for a minute," his father whispered. "I've got to get out of that living room for a while."

He reopened the bedroom door and called down the stairs, "James needs a little help with his arithmetic homework. I'll be back down in a while."

Quick on the uptake James chimed in, "Yeah. This new stuff is really hard and Dad can probably explain it better than Miss Witherspoon."

Father and son looked at each other with a grin. His father gave him a wink and tussled his hair as he closed the bedroom door.

"Thanks son. I owe you one."

"Three hundred and twenty nine," said James.

"I had to get out of there," said Charles. "There is only so much Millicent any man should have to take, and I think I reached that point sometime in July. She's down there harping at your mother, Doris and I because John had an accident when he was going out to help me last night. Still it made for a pretty funny story, but you know what would have happened if we had laughed."

Charles told James the whole story about the previous night's escapade. He explained the mistake the gas station attendant had made, the trip to the jail, and what really happened to their car. When he related the story that he had just heard about what had happened to John, both of them doubled over in quiet laughter. The last thing either of them wanted was to be heard laughing when they were supposedly working on James' arithmetic homework.

There's nothing funny about the twelve times table.

A noise outside drew James and Charles to the bedroom window. Outside in the Cooper Back yard, Mike Cooper was using his lawn roller to flatten a patch of snow where the Cooper Ice Arena would take shape. As he rolled, Coop was using a snow shovel to compress the snow around the edges into tightly packed walls.

"Looks like Coop's getting his skating rink started," said James trying hard not to sound hopeful.

He knew that his father was not going to build a skating rink in their backyard, and he decided that it was probably best not sounding like he was asking for one.

"I guess it'll look like the picture on my calendar when it's done," he added.

Charles walked over and looked at the calendar. The boys playing hockey all looked happy, with bright red cheeks. One of them had obviously just scored a goal, because he was holding his hockey stick over his head and grinning. Another boy, with newspapers tied around his legs was digging the puck out of a makeshift net.

Charles felt a little pang of guilt. He knew that in lots of ways he had no real understanding of what a father was supposed to do. He barely remembered

his own father, and his mother had not been the sort
of woman to attract potential stepfathers to their
door.

His social life was largely limited to dinners at
John and Millicent's house and they were hardly the
sort of people you would turn to, even if you did
want to admit you need some advice on dealing with
children. He wasn't sure that Mike Cooper was the
right sort of person to emulate either. He thought
that Coop Jr. got too much handed to him. He heard
the other men at the office talking about things they
did with their children, but he also was of the
opinion that most of them were what he called
"idiots, goofballs and nincompoops."

Once again the cellmate's words flooded into his
subconscious.

He looked at his son, staring out the window at
the Coopers' construction project. He really was a
good kid. He was responsible. You just had to look at
all the work he had done on the driveway the night
before to realize that. He did pretty well in school.

And he owed him one, or three hundred and
twenty nine.

"You know," he said, "I'm thinking that the back
lawn is going to need a lot of work next spring
anyway."

James spun on his heels. He wasn't sure if he was
hearing his father or if he was imagining what it
would be like to hear him say that.

"So, maybe on the weekend we could try our
hand at building a skating rink of our own out back."

"Really?" asked James, hoping beyond hope that
his father wasn't pulling his leg.

"Well, there'd be some conditions attached to it,"

Charles said. "You'd have to let Louise use it some of the time and I'd want you to help me teach Georgie how to skate."

"Sure," agreed James.

At this point he would have agreed to just about anything if it meant that he would have his very own skating rink in the backyard.

Father and son stood in silence for a few moments watching Mike Cooper smooth and compress the snow in his backyard.

"Well, I guess you should be pretty well finished your arithmetic by now," Charles finally said. "I'd better head back downstairs to your aunt and uncle. John should just about be finished with the sentence he was starting when I came up here by now."

James didn't bother suggesting that he join his father downstairs. He chose the safety of an entire evening in his own room over being trapped in the same room with Aunt Millicent for more than five minutes.

Every so often, he slipped to his listening post to hear what the adults were talking about. It seemed that they weren't doing much talking. Aunt Millicent didn't give the rest of them an opportunity. She controlled the conversation in every room she ever entered, much the way Louise had at the dinner table.

James suddenly realized that the reason his Uncle John talked so slowly was that he was constantly waiting for Millicent to interrupt him. He was afraid to move on the next word in case it came out over top of something Millicent was going to say over top of him.

Eventually, James heard the front door close and his mother's exasperated voice saying, "That woman…"

He took it as a sign that it might be safe to go downstairs and get a snack before getting ready for bed. When he got there, his mother seemed particularly disturbed.

"James," she said, "always remember that you are only related to that woman by marriage. And you, Charles Kelly, sneaking off upstairs like that and leaving me stuck alone with her."

James decided that it was probably safest to let his mother calm down for a while. She usually needed it after an evening with Millicent. He finished the cookie he was eating and headed upstairs to get ready for bed.

Charles wished he could do the same.

Chapter Eight

The Hill Of The Seven (Or Eight) Bumps

James woke early the next morning. More snow had fallen overnight, and his father was already outside clearing off the sidewalk and unplugging the driveway that Steve Murphy had filled in with the snow from the end of his plow blade.

The new Ford station wagon was parked in the driveway. James liked the look of the new car, but he still had the feeling that it was going to detract from whatever might land under the Kelly Christmas tree that year.

By the time he was washed and dressed, he could

hear his father coming back into the house.

His mother and Doris were puttering in the kitchen. James could smell the freshly brewed coffee and wondered why adults thought that stuff tasted good. He had tried a sip a few times, but could not bring himself to ever imagining that he would want a full cup. He poured himself a bowl of cereal and as he ate, he listened to the sounds of his father muttering about where he would like to put all the snow that Murphy had piled into the end of the driveway.

James imagined that it would probably be pretty uncomfortable for Steve Murphy to have all that snow shoved where his father was suggesting.

"I think Coop and I are going to go tobogganing after school today," James announced to no one in particular.

No one in particular responded, so James took that as an implied permission.

"Come home before you go," said his mother at last. "Since *someone* forgot to get you a new pair of galoshes at Clarkson's yesterday, I guess I will have to go down and get you a pair."

'Someone' did a lot of things around the Kelly household. It was Lorraine's way of letting Charles know that he had forgotten to do something that he should have without coming right out and naming him.

"Someone had a lot on his mind yesterday," said Charles, more to his coffee cup than to Lorraine.

Lorraine turned her attention to the piece of toast she was buttering for James and said to it, "Well, we all know it doesn't take too much to overfill someone's mind with details, don't we."

Had Charles and Lorraine not been grinning throughout the conversation one might have thought that they were not the happy couple that they were. The constant banter back and forth was the foundation that their marriage was built upon, and everyone, even three-year-old Georgie in his highchair, knew it and would only be worried if it stopped.

Like most Fridays, the school day dragged.

Miss Witherspoon's class spent the first part of the morning working on their arithmetic test. It was filled with multiplication and long division. The only sounds that disturbed the silence of the room were the occasional movement of a chair, a cough here or there, and the sounds of pencils writing and erasers erasing.

James wrote down the answer to the last question just as Miss Witherspoon announced it was time to turn in the papers. He didn't have time to go back over his answers, but he felt pretty confident that he had done everything correctly. Coop, on the other hand was still working feverishly, and from the look of his paper, James figured that he still had three or four questions that would go unanswered.

After recess, they turned their attention to a reading comprehension test. James liked reading and he found the test to be easy.

His spirits were high as he ran the two blocks

home for lunch. He hoped that he would have a good report card to show his parents when Miss Witherspoon handed them out on the last day of class before Christmas. It just might swing things a bit more in his favor, especially if, as he was now reasonably certain, Santa Claus was just a role played for your benefit by your parents.

Just inside the back door, James found a row of three new pairs of galoshes. He was relieved by the sight, because his feet were cold from the short run home and the galoshes would mean he'd be warm on the way back.

He got excited when he realized that those galoshes meant that his mother and Aunt Doris had spent the morning at Clarkson's Department Store. If he played his cards just right, he might be able to use the opportunity to drop some well-placed hints about electric trains.

James pulled up a chair at the kitchen table. Louise was ladling out bowls of tomato soup. A plate of grilled cheese sandwiches was set in the middle of the table.

"So I see you went to Clarkson's this morning Mom," said James as trying hard to sound as nonchalant as possible.

"Yes dear," said Lorraine as she put the bowl of soup in front of him. "I got you your new galoshes and did a little other shopping while I was there."

Well, did you happen to see the electric train display in the toy department," James asked hoping that an affirmative answer would open the door to further discussion of the merits of various cars, engines and track layouts.

"Oh no, James," said his mother. "By the time we got the galoshes and Aunt Doris got the wool she needed it was time to come home and make your lunch.

"Oh joy," thought James. "The raw material for another pair of Christmas socks."

James ate the rest of his meal in silence. He thought he had made some headway with his father when they had visited Clarkson's the day before, but obviously, his mother was going to be a harder nut to crack. As for Aunt Doris, he knew that she was a lost cause.

After two tests in the morning, Miss Witherspoon decided to let the children off with an easier afternoon. They usually had a spelling test on Friday afternoons, but she told them that it was postponed until Monday, an announcement that led to a round of cheers from the children and a look of relief to creep across Coop's face. He couldn't have faced a third test in one day.

Instead of spelling, she brought out more construction paper and the box filled with the tubes from toilet paper, paper towel and other similar products that she had been asking the children to contribute to all year. The project was to make stars for their Christmas trees or, in the case of Irv and Sadie, Stars of David for their Hanukkah celebration.

While the children worked on their art projects, Hilda Witherspoon marked the morning's tests.

From time to time, the children would hear her make a quiet "tsk" sound, indicating that some child had disappointed her with an answer on the test. Every child in the room hoped that theirs was not the test being marked.

When three-thirty finally arrived, the children were excited. Two days off to play in all that fresh snow was almost too good to be true. James and Coop raced home, with Louise trailing not far behind. She hoped that the boys would take her tobogganing with them, and if they didn't want to, she knew she could get her mother to make them take her.

James hoped he could simply drop off his books, grab the round aluminum 'flying saucer' sled he had gotten for his birthday last year, and hurry off to River Ravine Park before Louise would have a chance to get their mother to intercede on her behalf. She was not allowed to go to the park on her own because it meant crossing busy Steel Street at a traffic light. James' plan might have worked had the saucer not been buried in the snow behind the garage. As he dug it out, he vowed that he was going to start planning things better. If he had just gotten the saucer ready the night before, he could have been half a block from home before his sister got there.

"Take Louise with you, James."

He knew those words were coming as soon as he heard the back door open.

"And keep an eye on her."

He was about to protest, but he remembered just how close they were to Christmas. Taking his sister tobogganing might just be the kind of thing that could push his popularity over the top in the minds of parents who might be wavering on the topic of electric trains and such.

"Sure, Mom, I'll even dig out her sled for her."

He really hoped his mother was noticing all that cooperation.

River Ravine Park was two blocks north of Parkland Road. Most of the year it was just a quiet few acres, sloping down on both sides to a small creek. In the winter, it was a noisy, crowded playground filled with toboggans, sleds, and even a few garbage can lids that some kids used to glide down the best hill in the entire city - The Hill Of The Seven Bumps.

From top to bottom, snow sliding gear would traverse over seven bumps that ranged from one that was barely noticeable to one that sent gear and passengers flying, sometimes resulting in bumps bruises and broken limbs. Everyone who ever grew up within twenty-five blocks of River Ravine Park can still remember their first trip down the hill. It's etched into minds of children and adults and it became a rite of passage for most of them. When you were old enough to ride down the Hill Of The Seven Bumps you were well on your way to manhood or womanhood.

Flying saucers, like James' were new. They flew down the hill at breakneck speeds, but were virtually impossible to control once they had a bit of momentum. No one had ever tried to take a saucer down The Hill Of The Seven Bumps. The children who had them preferred the safety of the gentler slopes on either side.

"You'll have to use the kiddies' hill," James said

to Louise as they walked to the corner. "Coop and I are going on The Hill Of The Seven Bumps."

"That's not fair," she said, but her protests were just words. She didn't think she was quite brave enough for the big hill, so she acquiesced and headed to the south side of the park where she could sled with many of her classmates who had already arrived.

James and Coop stood atop the Hill of the Seven Bumps. Neither of them would admit it, but they both felt a slight twinge of panic as they looked at the other kids racing down the hill and becoming airborne after the notorious bump number four. If you hit number four just right, you could completely miss bumps five and six.

There was a short flat section of ground just before bump seven, which was actually the top of the bank of the small creek at the bottom of the ravine. It was a goal of every kid who ever rode the bumps to hit number seven perfectly and secure your place among those who felt the eighth bump, something that was only achieved by landing on the other side of the creek. Many a child had a long wet and cold walk home from River Ravine Park when their toboggan didn't clear the creek and broke through the ice. There were rumors of children who had drowned trying to clear the creek, but most people doubted that had ever happened. At its deepest during the spring runoff the creek might have been two feet deep. By the time winter arrived, just a few inches of water flowed below the ice.

Still, retelling stories of bloated bodies not found until springtime was a great way to add terror to a younger kid's first venture down The Hill Of The Seven Bumps.

The boys decided to play rock/paper/scissors to see who would get to go first. In both of their minds, they were actually playing to see who *had* to go first. Coop lost, or won, depending on how you looked at it, and slowly James set the flying saucer down at the top of the hill. He sat on it and waited a moment.

"What are you doing, James, praying or deciding to chicken out?" Coop taunted.

"I... I'm just trying to determine the scariest route to take," James replied, trying hard to sound brave, but failing miserably.

"Yeah, so he can take a different route," said one of the grade eight boys waiting to take his turn. "If you're too much of a fraidy-cat, you can always go to the kiddy hill on the other side of the park, besides, no one is dumb enough to try this hill on a flying saucer. Get out of our way and let the big kids show you how it's done."

James hesitated for another moment. Just as he was about to get off the saucer, Coop came up behind him and pushed him over the edge of the hill.

The saucer slowly spun, so that James was facing back up the hill. Coop and the older boys were standing still watching him careen toward the first bump. James held onto the two rope handles for all he was worth. He saw the other boys cringe, but before he could process what that might mean, he hit the first bump. The saucer lifted off the ground and spun around in the air.

James heard a loud scream. Before he realized that it was coming from his own mouth he hit bump two and was airborne again. The saucer spun faster and the world became a blur. It only touched down for an instant before hitting the third bump.

He was picking up speed as he crested the infamous bump four. It lifted off and this time he was airborne for what seemed like a very long time. He cleared bump five and was still in the air when he sailed over bump six. The boys at the top of the hill could see a foot of air between the top of the saucer and the bottom of James. It touched down followed shortly thereafter by James. Somehow he managed to hang on as he raced onward to bump seven. In no time, he was airborne again. Every kid on the hill was watching to see just how far he would go. Just when it seemed he was going to be the first fourth grader to successfully hit bump eight, the front of the saucer dipped slightly, causing a head on collision with the edge of the creek bank. It stopped instantly, but James did not. He continued in the air for another six feet landing with an audible thud at the base of the kiddies' hill just in time for Louise to reach to the bottom.

James rolled several times after he hit the ground, stopping just short of the front runners of Louise's sled. He lay staring up at the sky.

"Are you OK, James?" Louise asked. "You're saucer is down by the creek and you're all the way up here. Did you mean to do that, James?"

"No, yeah and no," mumbled James answering all of the girl's questions in as few words as possible.

At the top of the Hill of the Seven Bumps Coop wasn't too sure if he was very interested in following James down the hill. One thing was certain. If he did work up the courage, he was glad he'd be doing it on his toboggan, not a flying saucer. At last, he decided that, even if he wound up hurtling himself through the air the way James had, he really didn't have a choice in the matter. James and the rest of the school would never let him live it down if he didn't go down the hill. Using his hands to propel the toboggan, he pushed himself to the edge of the hill and started down.

Bumps one through three were jarring, but not too hard to take. When Coop hit bump four, he lifted off, but the toboggan provided more wind drag than the streamlined saucer. He cleared bump five, but landed just ahead of bump six which jarred him free of the toboggan. He rolled off and it continued alone until it came to a stop in the creek bed behind what was left of James bent and mangled saucer.

Coop got up, dusted the snow off his coat and pants, and walked over to his still prone friend.

"You OK, James?" he asked echoing Louise's words.

"I think I'd just like to go home," James murmured. "You guys can stay here if you want. I'll understand."

"No," said Coop, almost relieved that he wouldn't have to take another run down the hill. "We'll walk home with you to make sure you're OK."

Coop helped James get to his feet. He was feeling guilty for sending his friend over the edge of the hill. James was a little wobbly, but managed to stay upright. He had snow driven down the inside his coat and some of it was melting, causing icy rivers to flow down his back and into his pants. He limped slightly as they walked to gather up their belongings.

Coop put the remains of the saucer on top of his toboggan and Louise's sled on top of that to hold it down and pulled them all back together.

"You weren't gone long," Lorraine said when the children came back into the house.

"I had a bit of an accident on The Hill Of The Twenty-seven Bumps," said James weakly.

"It's just seven bumps," reminded his mother.

"Not the way I took it today," said James.

Chapter Nine

Un-Charleslike Behavior

James headed up to his room to recuperate from his wild ride at the park. He lay on his bed, while Louise went to the kitchen to help their mother with dinner preparations. He left his door open so he could hear anything interesting that might be going on in the rest of the house.

After a few minutes, he heard his father in the hall downstairs dialing the phone. James slipped to his 'listening post' to hear if his call might have something to do with Christmas.

Charles was talking to someone in a business like tone. James heard him say, "Yes. I know there's probably not a lot there, but I've had an upheaval at work, and I need to borrow whatever I can against my policy to see me through until I find something new."

James wasn't sure what it meant, but since it didn't seem to involve Christmas or electric trains, he tried to put it out of his mind and went back to his room. As he lay on the bed, his father's words repeated in his mind. James wondered what he meant by "an upheaval at work" and why that would mean he needed money. He hoped that it had something to do with the car, but he still felt a sense of unease over what he had heard.

James woke up early on Saturday morning. The house was quiet. He'd forgotten about his father's strange telephone conversation of the night before. He could hear Charles snoring in his parent's bedroom. Georgie was asleep in his crib. Louise was awake and playing with one of her dolls on her bed. Downstairs, Doris slept soundly. James always avoided looking into the room that had been converted into a bedroom for her. The sight of her false teeth resting at the bottom of a glass of water always unnerved him.

James went to the kitchen and served himself a bowl of cereal. He was still limping a bit from his unceremonious ride down the Hill Of The Seven Bumps, but he was excited about the day ahead, and hoped that his father hadn't forgotten about their plans to build a backyard skating rink.

Charles had taught the children to avoid coming into the master bedroom to wake their parents. James developed a method of his own to wake his father on the important days like Christmas morning, and he decided that the prospect of building a skating rink made this an important enough day to use the trick.

He went into the bathroom and flushed the toilet. Throughout the house pipes erupted in a series of thumps and other noises. When they quieted and the toilet tank was once again filled, he flushed again...

And again...

And again.

The water made its way into the Kelly house through a meter that the city used to determine how much of Charles' income should be sent to them for water usage. It was a bill that Charles particularly disliked. He didn't think people should be charged for something that falls from the sky for free.

Normally he would awaken by the third or fourth flush. Sometimes it had been known to take as many as eight. The result was always the same. Charles would hear the water flowing and the pipes rattling and would eventually be conscious enough to realize that it was going on for longer than it should have.

"Dammit all we're on a water meter," were the first words the boy would hear from his father on those special days.

"Works like a charm," thought James, who would then sneak back to his own room and be back in bed by the time his father would get to the hall.

It was close to eleven o'clock before father and

son trudged through the snow into the back yard towing the old cement lawn roller that had been in the garage when Charles inherited the house. The overcast skies that dumped so much snow on the city had been replaced by clear blue, and the temperature had dropped by several degrees.

Charles looked over the fence at the Cooper's rink to get an idea of the size of lawn he'd be destroying with this project. Turning over a new leaf and paying more attention to his family was one thing. Destroying more lawn than was absolutely necessary was quite another.

He took a shovel and outlined an area roughly the same size and shape as his neighbor's. He then traced the outline with the roller. It was hard going. The roller was heavy enough without the extra resistance the snow was providing. It wasn't long before he started to feel his shirt dampening with sweat from all the exertion, despite the cold temperature. While Charles rolled the snow flat, James compressed the snow around the edges with the shovel the way he had seen Coop doing it a couple of nights before.

Mike Cooper heard the noise coming from the Kelly's back yard and looked out to see what was going on. He could scarcely believe his eyes. There was good old Charlie-boy acting very unCharlie-boyish, actually willingly damaging his precious lawn to build a skating rink for his children.

"Jeanie, I see it, but I don't believe it," he said to his wife. "Charlie's out there building a skating rink. I don't think he really has a clue about what he's doing."

Those last words were out of his mouth before he had a chance to stop himself. He knew as soon as he said that what Jean would say to him. He even mouthed along with her while she said it.

"Well, you really should go out there and help him don't you think?"

It wasn't really a question. It was clear to Mike that he had better get himself out the door if he knew what was good for him.

Mike pulled his much newer and lighter lawn roller out of the garage, and dragged it clanging and banging up the Kelly's driveway. Charles heard the noise and stopped pushing his roller. He wasn't sure what it was, but at that point, he'd take just about any excuse to take a break from flattening the snow.

"Hey, Charlie-boy. Thought you could use a hand," Mike called as he came through the Kelly's gate. "I brought along my experience and expertise in rink building, too."

Charles was more than a little bit relieved. He knew he had to get the snow flattened and he had to pour water onto the compressed snow afterwards, but he had to admit that he was in a bit over his head as far as how to do it properly. Mike Cooper was exactly what he needed right then.

"Get rid of that concrete monstrosity you're trying to shove around," said Mike. "I'll finish up rolling the snow and you get your hose connected and out here."

By the time Charles found his hose and carried it out to the back yard, Mike was almost finished his last pass with the roller. He had covered more ground in a few minutes that Charles had managed in half an hour.

James had ignored the two men, putting all of his concentration into compressing the edges of the rink. His imagination was running at full speed. He saw himself as a great National Hockey League player skating down the ice, tossing hapless opponents out of his way as he single handedly led his team to victory. The thought of his team reminded him that he hadn't seen Coop that morning.

"Where's Coop, I mean Mike Junior, Mr. Cooper," he asked.

"Mike's working on the train set downstairs. He's hoping Santa will bring him some more accessories for it. You and your dad should come over and see it when we're done here."

James gave his father a questioning look. Charles nodded and winked back.

Mike Sr. went back to his yard, pulled his hose to the fence and tossed the business end over to the Kelly side. For the next half hour, the two men sprayed a fine mist of water over the compressed snow until a puddle nearly an inch deep filled the square outline of the rink.

"I feel like I've picked up a bit of a chill, Charlie-boy," Mike said as they drained the hoses and coiled them.

It was Mike's way of suggesting that Charles might have some form of liquid in the house that could get rid of the chill.

"So you want a cup of coffee, then Mike?" Charles asked, knowing full well that coffee was not anywhere near the top of Mike's list of wants.

"Well, I supposed it could be served in a coffee cup," said Mike with a grin. "I brought that bottle we started at the dealership home. It might warm us up a bit and James can see the train set.

The two men headed for the back door of the Cooper's house. James stood watching the pool of water in what he had hoped he'd be skating on that same day.

He called to the men, "When will it be ready to skate on?"

"It'll probably be Monday or Tuesday before it's all finished, James. We have to add a lot more layers of ice before it can handle you and your friends skating on it," Mike explained.

"Monday or Tuesday," thought James. "I thought I'd be playing hockey this afternoon."

He stood and watched the pool of water for a few minutes longer, hoping to see some sign that it was freezing a lot faster than his father predicted. The water was not showing any sign of cooperating, so James decided to go next door and warm up with his father and Mr. Cooper. Before leaving the yard, he shoveled a path from the rink to the back door, so that it would be ready as soon as the ice was finished.

Mike poured healthy triple shots of scotch into highball glasses to help get rid of the chill. He instructed Charles and James to follow him down to the basement.

They could hear the sound of the trains as soon as Mike opened the basement door. When they got downstairs both Kellys were surprised by the intricate layout that filled half of the Cooper basement, and almost rivaled the display at Clarkson's Department Store.

Coop sat at on a high stool, watching the trains, adjusting the speed controls and switching the tracks so that they would take different routes through the display. He was wearing a gray and blue engineer's hat. Mike Sr. sat down on a stool beside his son and put on a matching hat. James looked at the display in awe. Charles watched the interaction between the two Coopers, wishing that he could do the same with James. The father and son were clearly enjoying each other's company, and keenly interested in the way the trains moved around the tracks.

Eventually, Mike Sr. stood up and motioned James to take his place on the stool. He took of his cap and placed it on James' head.

"Let's leave these two railway tycoons down here and go up and refill our glasses, Charlie-boy," he said, heading for the stairs.

Mike brought the glasses into the living room and said, "You should get James a train set like ours, Charles. We get more enjoyment out of that thing, and it gives us a lot of time together."

Charles was a bit envious of the fun his neighbor must have with his son, not that James wouldn't enjoy it too, but Charles felt he was out of his league when it came to knowing how to be a father.

"I'd like to, Mike, but I just can't swing it this year, not with everything that is going on with the car and everything else," he said, staring into his drink.

"Don't make excuses Charlie-boy," Mike said, sounding a bit annoyed. "Kids need to be kids, and they need us to be kids with them."

Charles wondered what it was like to be a kid. His mother had forced him to be a little adult from the time he could remember.

"But the car…" Charles started.

"Look," Mike said, now sounding really annoyed. "Is this some kind of a game to make me take more money off the offer I gave you?"

"No…no." Charles protested. "You made me a great offer, I just don't think I can afford it or much of anything else right now."

Charles looked around the room, making sure no one was close by. "Mike," he said, "I haven't even told Lorraine this yet, but I lost my job the other day. The company sent in a guy from head office and he closed our whole department. He said something about contracting the work out to save money. I don't know what I'm going to do. I can't afford the car, but I need a car. I can't afford a train set. I don't even know how I'm going to pay the bills in a month or so, without completely stripping all our savings."

Mike stood up. "Drink your drink, Charlie-boy, I'll be back in a minute."

Charles stared down at his glass. "I seem to be left staring at a lot of liquids lately," he thought.

He didn't know why he had blurted out his secret to Mike, even before telling Lorraine. As soon as he said it, he was sorry he had. Charles was not the sort of man who, at the best of times, could share things easily. These were certainly not the best of times, so why was he able to tell Mike about it, now.

Mike came back into the room carrying a pad.

He looked at Charles and said, "OK, Charlie-boy. Jenny and I have talked it over. Here's what we're going to do about all this. Jenny has been doing the books for the dealership ever since my bookkeeper got pregnant and moved away. Frankly, and if you tell her I said this I'll deny it, she's lousy at it. My accountant is going to have a coronary when I give him the books come April if I don't get things sorted out. So on the Monday after New Year's you'll start working for me down at the dealership. Forget about the car. It's now your company car. We'll start you off at $125.00 a week and look at it again in a few months."

Charles entered a shock-like state. He didn't know what to say, which was probably just as well, because he didn't think he could remember how to make his mouth work. A tear started to well up in his eye, and it took all his strength to prevent it from opening a floodgate.

"I... I... don't know what to say, Mike," he started, thinking he sounded like his brother-in-law trying to get a sentence out in his slow methodical way.

"Now don't start negotiating with me here, Charlie-boy," Mike said with a grin.

"No!" Charles said, perhaps a little too vehemently. He wouldn't have even thought of negotiating. That was $25.00 a week more than he was making at the office he had spent fifteen years being loyal to, so he didn't feel he was in any position to negotiate.

"I mean, I don't know how to thank you, Mike," he finally stammered.

"Well, you can start by paying a bit more attention to the things that boy of yours likes," Mike said. "I feel a bit guilty seeing what I give Mike Jr., and I know I probably spoil him more than I should, but James is a good kid, and you should recognize and reward that."

"Well, in that case, I have another favor to ask, Mike," Charles whispered.

"You're getting pretty good at it," replied Mike with a grin as he raised his glass in salute.

"Seriously," Charles continued, "I guess it's obvious that I haven't always been the best at paying attention to details around here. I had already decided that it was time to make some changes. I realized that I don't want James to look back on his childhood the way I look back on mine. That's why I said I'd let him have the skating rink this year. It's time I started being a bit more involved in the family, and a little less worried about money."

"I wish you'd told me that earlier," laughed Mike. "I wouldn't have offered you a hundred and a quarter."

"Well, it's all got me thinking; that and my little run-in with the police the other night." Charles said, still making sure he wasn't speaking loudly enough to be heard outside the room. "I see the way you are with your wife and kids, and to be honest Mike, I'm a little envious. Maybe if I started doing some of the things you do with your family, I can get my life more on track."

Mike Cooper had never heard Charles like this before. He was actually opening up, something that men - especially men like Charles - weren't supposed to do. He could see that Charles was trying in his own awkward way, to make sense of his life and improve in some areas that he could certainly use improvement.

"Look, Mike," Charles said. "You said it yourself, we've always helped each other out, our wives are best friends and our kids alternate from being best friends to mortal enemies, but under the surface they really are close. I saw how you and Mike Jr. were enjoying that train set, and I see you out there building snowmen with your kids to advertise the car dealership. I can just imagine what most of the neighbors, let alone my family, would do if I went outside to build a snowman with James, Louise and Georgie."

Mike laughed at the thought of seeing Charles, good old dyed in the wool Charlie-boy, building a snowman.

"So, other than giving you a job, providing you with a car and helping you with your skating rink, where do I come into this grand scheme of yours," he said as he finished the last sip of his drink.

"OK," Charles started, "When I was a kid, Christmas was always the time you got what you needed, not what you might have wanted. It just happened year after year. Except for the two old eccentric aunts I had who took it upon themselves to try to rescue me from time to time, I could always count on getting clothes and maybe some book that my mother thought I needed to read. It was probably pretty much the same for Lorraine being raised by her mother and old Doris. As a result, Christmas around here looks pretty much the same as it did for us as kids."

Mike realized that this was possibly going to be a long conversation. He held up his glass and showed Charles its lack of meaningful contents. Charles didn't miss the hint. He took a long gulp from his drink and let it sooth his throat before letting Mike pour them each anther round.

"So I was wondering if you'd mind coming down to Clarkson's with me and help me pick out a train set for James," he said, and then sat back in his chair to wait for an answer.

"That's it?" asked Mike. "With all this big buildup I thought you were going to ask me something hard. Sure, I suppose I could do that, but there'd be a fee of course. We'd have to make a stop at O'Malley's while we were down there."

Charles laughed, partially at the thought that Mike would think to ask him to buy him a drink at the tavern down the street from Clarkson's and partially out of relief that he was willing to help him with his first real Christmas shopping.

The two men sat back in silence for a few minutes and let the scotch warm their throats and thoughts. Charles once again realized just how lucky he really was between having his family and a friend like Mike Cooper. Mike was wondering if Charles had just temporarily lost his mind, or if he really did want to change.

When he'd finished his drink Mike sat up and said, "Well, Charlie-boy, let's get this conspiracy in motion. I'll go and tell Jeanie what we're up to and meet you out by your garage in ten minutes."

Charles entered the house through the back door. He came into the kitchen, where Lorraine was baking Christmas cookies. He tried to sneak one off a hot cookie sheet and was smacked across the fingers with a lifter for his efforts.

"Oh no you don't, Charles Kelly," Lorraine said with a smile belying her stern tone. "Those are for company."

"Ah yes," Charles said grinning, "You want to have plenty of holiday cheer around for your favorite sister-in-law. Listen, Mike and I are going downtown. He needs some help with some Christmas shopping. We'll be back in a while."

He didn't like lying to Lorraine, but he was planning a surprise for her, too. She'd never suspect that he was the one doing the Christmas shopping.

Lorraine lifted four star-shaped cookies from one of the cooling racks and slipped them into a small brown bag. "A little something for the trip," she said and gave Charles a kiss on the cheek.

As Charles was heading out the door, James was just coming in. He'd been outside with Coop, checking the progress of the skating rink. His cheeks were bright red from the cold air.

"Where you going, Dad?" the boy asked, hoping that seeing his father in his coat and boots meant that it was time to do some more work on the rink.

"Mr. Cooper and I have an errand to run," his father said. "We'll take a look at the rink when I get back. Maybe, in the meantime, you and Mike Jr. can do some Christmas wishing together while we're gone."

"Right," thought James. "Do I wish for black socks or brown ones?"

❀ ❀ ❀

James watched his father and Mike Cooper drive down Parkland Road towards the traffic light at the corner. Something seemed different about his father and it wasn't just the new car or the sudden change of heart about building a backyard skating rink. He wasn't sure if he should be worried about it and probably would have spent some time thinking it through, but he smelled the cookies and that aroma took his full attention.

He walked to the kitchen window and looked out at the back yard and the partially completed skating rink. It was all a ruse to get his mother's attention away from the rack of cookies that was cooling on the counter between the oven and the sink.

"Did you see how much we got done on The Kelly Forum out back, Mom?" he asked hoping to get her to come to the window.

Lorraine Kelly smiled, knowing that her son planned to scoop up a couple of cookies as soon as she had her back turned from the rack, and she played along with the game. She walked to the window and looked out, giving James his opportunity. Before she could turn around James had two large sugar cookies palmed and was heading for the kitchen door.

Lorraine turned and called after him, "The rest of these cookies are for company, young man."

"Yeah, I know," said James, "You're really looking forward to Aunt Millicent coming over to eat them, aren't you?"

Lorraine shook her head. "Just like his father..."

James sat in the living room and ate the cookies. He picked up the Clarkson's Christmas catalog and started thumbing through the pages, carefully avoiding the dog-eared pages that Louise had been perusing for the past several days. The last thing he wanted was for anyone, even a member of his own family to see him looking at the catalog and accidentally be on a page filled with dolls and accessories.

He finally found the page he was looking for. Thundering across it was the powerful locomotive of the deluxe electric train set. It was pulling a coal car, several boxcars, and a caboose around an oval track. Small buildings lined the tracks. Each item on the page had a large letter beside it that corresponded to the description of the item on the opposite page.

James looked at the train set for a long time, imagining that he was in control of its every movement as it shunted back and forward putting together a full load of cars for the long trip across the country. He turned to the description.

> "Clarkson's is proud to present our biggest and most exciting electric train set yet. The C210 locomotive thunders down the track layout with real smoke coming from its stack. As it approaches the road crossing section of track, warning bells sound and its whistle loudly warns passersby that it is coming. Complete with four cars, a coal tender, caboose, station, trees, people and switches. Also included is an incredible seventeen feet of track, enough to build your whole main line and a siding using the two specially designed

> *switches. It's every boy's dream all*
> *wrapped up in a box."*

They were right. It was the dream of just about every boy in Miss Witherspoon's class to wake up on Christmas morning and find that particular item under the tree. James knew that it was just a dream. He knew the likelihood of that train arriving in the Kelly household was thinner than the sheet of ice he saw forming on the water in the rink just before he came in. When he looked at the price he concluded that, if he saved all of his allowance, he might have enough to buy it for himself when he was twenty-one years old.

James closed the book. He decided that it was probably better to stop looking at things he wasn't likely to ever get, and resign himself to opening brightly wrapped packages containing Aunt Doris's scratchy homemade wool socks, a few new packages of underwear, and maybe a shirt or a pair of pants.

The Christmas holidays were still something to look forward to, especially now that he had his own skating rink. Coop could come over and skate with him leaving the rink in his yard to his older sister and her eighth grade friends. One thing that was certain was that he didn't have much interest in a return visit to the Hill Of The Seven Bumps anytime soon.

There'd be lots of good food, candy and other treats over the holidays. His mother and her aunt would probably spend every day between now and Christmas Eve cooking up a storm. He hoped she remembered to make the little chocolate balls rolled in coconut that he liked so much, and the ginger cookies, and all the other baked goods that made

Lorraine Kelly famous all along Parkland Road.

Now that the Kellys had a new car, they'd be certain to go for a drive to look at the Christmas lights and displays around town. Lorraine Kelly always enjoyed that particular tradition, especially when Charles would turn down The Bridal Path, a road lined with the houses of the richest families in town. Each seemed determined to outdo the other in creating the greatest display of electrical consumption in reds, greens, blues, and yellows. James liked the event too, not so much because of the lights but because the evening always ended with a visit to the little delicatessen where a kindly old Mrs. Feldstein would pour large mugs of rich, dark hot chocolate. She always made a special fuss over James and insisted that it was an accident that his mug somehow got two marshmallows.

"I should charge extra for the boy's mug," she would say to Charles, "but I suppose you'd say it's entirely my fault that the extra marshmallow fell into it, so I'll let it pass… just this once."

Mrs. Feldstein had been letting it pass "just this once" ever since James could first recall going into her delicatessen.

Before James knew what was happening, the fresh air and exertion of the morning's work caught up with him and he fell asleep on the couch thinking about the taste of the hot chocolate and marshmallows.

❀ ❀ ❀

Charles pulled the new Ford Squire up to the curb in front of Clarkson's store. The street was filled with shoppers hurrying from one store to another, hoping that they could get their holiday shopping done on this last Saturday before Christmas.

Christmas carols blared out over speakers hung beneath the eaves of Clarkson's, beckoning customers away from the other shops. The front window display had been turned into a magical winter scene with mechanical deer bobbing their heads and rabbits twirling around on skates in time with a chipmunk choir singing in the background.

Charles didn't stop to look at the window. He was a man on a mission.

Mike Cooper followed Charles into the department store, stopping to throw some loose change into the kettle beside a man dressed as Santa Claus who was loudly shouting, "Ho Ho Ho" and ringing a bell.

The two men headed straight for the noisiest corner of the store, filled with children waiting in line to see the Santa Claus sitting on his golden throne in the corner, surrounded by the many aisles dedicated to Clarkson's Toyland.

The electric train display was still attracting a large crowd of boys and fathers alike. The salesman spotted Charles and remembered him for two days earlier.

"I had a feeling that one would be back," he thought.

Charles and Mike stood and watched the trains going through their delicate ballet of stops and starts, blowing their whistles and billowing small clouds of smoke from the locomotive stacks. It had the same hypnotic effect on the two men as it had on Charles on his previous visit.

Finally, Mike turned to his neighbor and said, "So Charlie-boy, are we here to buy a train set for James, or are you hoping Santa will bring one down your chimney for you?"

"Maybe a little of both," Charles said, grinning sheepishly.

"Well, you could start him off with a basic set, but I wouldn't recommend that. The trains just go around in an endless circle isn't very much fun. You'll want to set up a table like the one I have for Mike Junior, so that the train can actually do something." Mike said.

"I suppose you're right," Charles replied. He had vowed he wasn't going to worry too much about the price of the train set, but he hadn't considered the need for a table in his planning.

"What if I mounted a sheet of plywood on a couple of old sawhorses that I have downstairs?" he asked.

"Well," Mike replied, "that would work and it would probably give you plenty of room for expansion. That's one of the things I like about these trains. It takes a lot of the pressure out of shopping for birthday gifts and such. There's always something new you can add to the set."

Charles went to the shelves and looked at the various sets. Mike was right. They started with a pretty basic set with a round track, a locomotive one boxcar and a caboose, and went all the way up to the deluxe set that James had seen in the catalog. Charles decided that if he was going to do this properly, he might as well start with the deluxe set. He pulled a box off the shelf and started to walk back down the aisle toward the cash register. That's when the salesman made his move.

"Buying your boy the deluxe electric train, are you," he said. "It's a good start, but I'd recommend you take a look at the accessories aisle. You'll probably see a few things that you'd like to buy if you really want to make your son's Christmas."

Charles dutifully turned the corner following the direction the salesman was pointing. The accessories aisle was filled with buildings, sets of people, cars, tunnels, track and switches.

Charles added eight other boxes on top of the one he was already carrying. He had a sawmill with a dumping log car, a collection of people, cars and trees, several additional pieces of track, and two rolls of green felt to cover the sheet of plywood that would serve as the train table to the pile before heading to the cash register.

On the way, he passed the doll department.

"Oh my gosh," he said to Mike. "I almost forgot about Louise."

Sitting at the front of the doll department was a large dollhouse that opened to show several rooms, each lit with tiny electric lights.

"Grab one of those for me, would you Mike?" he said pointing to the dollhouse.

"Oh sure," joked Mike. "That's what I'm here for. Just call me your personal porter."

He wasn't sure whether it would be wise to remind his neighbor that he had a third child. Who knew what the sudden transformation would lead him to buy for Georgie? Whatever it would be, Mike saw himself trying to carry it, and he was struggling enough trying to carry the dollhouse through the crowded store. He decided he'd wait, at least until they had loaded the first batch of toys into the car.

Charles pulled out his checkbook and started to prepare the check while the clerk rang up the items on the cash register. Charles felt his knees buckle a little when she read the total to him, but he was determined to make this Christmas different, so he dutifully filled in the amount and handed her the check. There was only the slightest hesitation to let go of the check when she tried to take it from between his fingers.

As they loaded the toys into the car, Mike slapped Charles on the back.

"It's a good thing you've got the Squire, Charlie-boy," he said with a grin. "So, where are you planning on keeping all this stuff until Christmas?"

"Geez," Said Charles, suddenly realizing that he had a problem that he hadn't anticipated. "Could I store them at your place?"

"Well, you could," said Mike, but Junior is a notorious present hunter. The dollhouse might confuse him a bit. Why don't we take all this stuff and keep it in the closet in my office at the dealership. That's where I store my kids' presents. We could even stop off and pick up whatever you have for Georgie at home."

"Georgie!" shouted Charles. "I've forgotten about Georgie."

Charles asked Mike to stay with the car while he ran back into the store. A few moments later, he reemerged carrying three large boxes. The pictures on the sides made it clear that Georgie would be getting a bright yellow dump truck, a crane, and a road grader from Santa Claus.

"He'll probably spend more time playing with the boxes," said Charles.

Charles knew he had a bigger problem than where to hide the toys. He'd have to explain his purchases to Lorraine, and he wasn't entirely certain how she would react.

In their twelve years of marriage, they had not had a lot of time to themselves. Charles mother lived with them until she passed away just before Georgie arrived. Her room barely had a chance to be cleaned before Lorraine's Aunt Doris moved in with them. Charles loved his wife, but at times, he wasn't sure how well he knew her. A couple needed privacy for that, and that had been an unusual commodity during their marriage. Now that three children and an equal number of adults populated the house, it was barely possible to get a few minutes of privacy of his own, let alone with Lorraine.

After dropping the gifts off at Mike's office, the two men drove home. They decided to forego the stop at the pub, although Mike insisted that he would hold Charles to the agreement on another, less frantic day.

Charles thanked Mike for all his help and left him at the end of his driveway before returning to his own home. He sat in the car for several minutes enjoying the new car smell and listening to Christmas carols on the radio. He was lost in his own thoughts when there was a tap on the passenger window.

Loraine opened the door and said, "So what's a girl have to do to get asked to go for a ride in this new car, Mr. Kelly."

She sat down and slid across to the middle of the front seat to be close to her husband. Charles pretended to start an imaginary taximeter on the dash.

"Where to, Ma'am?" he asked, doffing his hat.

"Well, I could sure use a cup of coffee, if you know someone who'd like to buy me one," she replied.

"Your wish is my command," said Charles, enjoying the banter.

Charles put the car in reverse and backed out of the driveway. They drove to Mrs. Feldstein's deli and parked in the back. When they walked in the old woman grinned.

"What's this, already?" she asked. "The two of you alone, without a single child or in-law in tow. It must be a special occasion. If you'd called ahead I would have put out a table cloth."

"No occasion, Sadie," Lorraine said. "This rich man with a fancy new car has just offered to buy me a cup of coffee, and you know how easy it is to swoop me off my feet."

"Oy!" the older woman said. "Young love and in my deli, already."

The mention of being a rich man made Charles cringe inside. He still hadn't told Lorraine about the job, and he wasn't exactly sure how he was going to yet. Still, in a strange way, he was feeling richer than he had ever felt in is life, and only part of that was monetary.

Charles and Lorraine took a table by the front window. The winter afternoon light was quickly giving way to dusk, and colored lights were starting to appear along the eaves of the houses and stores up and down the street.

"This is nice," Lorraine said. "I can't remember the last time we went out for a coffee. Like Sadie says, even if we do we probably have the children or Doris with us, and it's just not the same."

"I have a confession to make," said Charles.

"Aha!" said Lorraine with a broad smile. "You really did punch me in the car the other night and used the fact that I was unconscious from the anesthesia to get away with it."

"No, nothing quite that dramatic," Charles said. His ego was still slightly bruised from the events of Wednesday night, and he wasn't quite ready to joke about them.

Charles held up his hand and said, "Lorraine, this is serious, but it has a happy ending I think. I need you to just let me tell you the whole thing without interruptions."

Lorraine looked a bit worried, but nodded her agreement to his wishes.

"On Wednesday, while you were at the dentist's office, I had to go back to work. There was a meeting with a guy who was there from head office to talk to us. To make a long story short, they're closing my department, and they let us all go. I'm not really taking vacation right now. I'm unemployed."

Lorraine's hand started to tremble and she had to set her coffee cup down to avoid spilling it. She felt tears welling up in her eyes, but didn't speak.

"I didn't know how to tell you, and I was trying to work it all out. I took out a small loan on my life insurance to make sure we'd be OK for money until I found something."

The tears were flowing down Lorraine's cheeks now. Charles couldn't look at her, because he wanted to get the whole story out.

"But the thing is, and this is the happy ending part, I talked with Mike Cooper this morning after we worked on the skating rink. I don't know why I came to tell him about all this, but it turns out he needs a new bookkeeper down at the dealership and he offered me $125.00 a week to come work for him. That's $25.00 more than I made before."

Lorraine wiped her eyes. "Seriously..." she said, almost afraid to believe that a story that started out so badly could end up so well.

"So," Charles continued, "About that confession I have to make to you..."

"That wasn't it?" Lorraine asked, almost afraid to think what might be coming next.

"Well, no," Charles started, "you'll probably be really upset about this."

Tears started forming in Lorraine's eyes as she started imagining the worst.

"But, well, it's just that when Mike and I went out today, I was the one who went Christmas shopping."

"Well I hope you bought me something nice and expensive," Lorraine teased.

"No... I mean not yet... Rather, I haven't done

any shopping for you yet," he stammered.

"I'm teasing," Lorraine said. "I bought myself a new coat the other day with money I had saved from the grocery budget. You can wrap that up for me."

Charles realized that his wife didn't have very high expectations when it came to getting gifts. It was the first time he had seen it for what it was, and he felt ashamed that he hadn't been more attentive to her in the past.

"I went shopping for the kids," he continued. "I bought James an electric train, Louise a big doll house and Georgie some big trucks for the sandbox."

"Oh I just bet you did," said Lorraine, clearly thinking that her husband was kidding. Nothing she had ever seen in their marriage could have prepared her for that to be the truth.

"Seriously, Lorraine," said Charles. "I want to make some changes for the kids and let them have some of the things their friends have. You've seen James' face whenever he mentions Coop's electric train set, and how often do we have to hear Louise recite the Clarkson's catalog before we get the idea she's just copying what her classmates are asking their parents for?"

Lorraine was surprised to hear Charles talk this way. It was certainly something very new for him. She was also secretly pleased. She had often felt a bit guilty when she saw the look of disappointment in her children's eyes at opening a brightly wrapped package of underwear, but she felt that Charles would never go for spending too much at Christmas, especially after her experience of living with his mother during the early years of their marriage.

"Lorraine, we have the money, even more now.

Let's just enjoy it for a change." Charles continued, still thinking that he had to convince her.

"Who are you, and what have you done with my husband?" she asked, as she reached across the table and clasped his hand.

At ten, James was still too young to babysit his brother and sister. Still, he was occasionally left taking care of them while his mother and her aunt were busy with other things. Doris was in her room with the door closed. She told James to keep an eye on his siblings while she worked on Christmas presents. He knew that it meant she wanted to be away from the children for a while and that she would be sitting in her room with her knitting, and a glass filled with red wine.

On this occasion, his mother and father were not around either, so he went to his sister's room to see what she was doing.

Louise had conscripted Georgie to take part in one of her doll tea parties. The youngest Kelly child was sitting at the little table in her room, happy to be in the company of his older sister, and even happier that she had snuck down to the kitchen and brought them each one of the cookies their mother had been baking.

"Want to have a bit of fun?" he said to her. "We're on our own."

Louise looked at her brother and her face brightened. She knew exactly what he meant. Having fun when they were on their own meant plotting new ways to play jokes on their youngest sibling. Georgie was still too young to realize what they were doing, and enjoyed the attention from his older brother and sister.

"Let's teach him the Christmas songs the kids are singing in the playground at recess," suggested James.

"Do you mean the rubber cigar one and stuff?" asked Louise.

"Sure that's a good one," replied her brother. "Do you want to learn a Christmas song for Santa, Georgie?"

"Santa's coming soon," said the boy, getting excited at the prospect.

"OK, now repeat after Louise and me. We three kings of orient are…" James instructed singing the tune along with his sister.

Georgie did his best to mimic them, "We thwee kings of owient are."

"Good, Georgie, good," said Louise. "Now repeat the next line. Trying to light a rubber cigar."

"Twying to wight a wubber cigaw," Georgie warbled.

"OK, now this is the hard part, Georgie, do you think you're big enough to sing this part?" James said trying hard not to laugh.

"I'm big!" Georgie proclaimed.

James and Louise sung the next line together, "It was loaded and exploded. Now we're on yonder star."

Georgie repeated the line as best he could, "It

was woaded and expwoaded. Now we on yondy staw."

The children spent the next half hour practicing the song with Georgie. They hoped he'd sing it at some inopportune moment, preferably when Aunt Millicent was around. She would be horrified. Before they could teach him another song, they heard the new car pulling into the driveway.

"We'll teach him the new version of Jingle Bells later," James told Louise. He then turned to his brother and said, "Let's not sing it for Mom and Dad yet. Let's wait until we've practiced some more. OK, Georgie?"

"OK," the younger boy said, excited about the prospect of more songs with his older brother and sister.

Lorraine Kelly was a very organized woman. She spent the morning baking Christmas cookies, and she prepared dinner ahead of time. Before starting her baking, she had thrown together the ingredients for stew into a pot that had simmered all day, adding its aroma to the sweet smells of the baking. When she and Charles returned from their drive, she simply set the table and served dinner.

Everything seemed in order. After dinner, she organized the children's baths. While she dried Georgie and put him to bed, Louise took her turn in the tub. Lorraine stayed and washed the young girl's hair, listening throughout the entire process to the litany of things the young girl had picked out to ask Santa for, all from pages eighteen through twenty-four of the Clarkson's Christmas catalog.

James would take his bath alone. After she finished drying Louise's hair and tucking her into bed, she stepped into her son's room to tell him that the time for his turn in the tub had arrived. The boy was on his bed, leafing through the pages of the catalog.

"Anything interesting in there, James?" she asked.

"Oh, yeah," James said, trying hard to sound noncommittal. "I guess the new car is going to be the gift for the whole family to enjoy this year, though."

"Well you never know what surprises Santa might have up his sleeve," she said.

"I think I'm getting too old for Santa Claus, Mom," James said. "Most of the other kids at school have figured out that it's just your parents pretending for the little kids' sake."

Lorraine was saddened to see that her oldest was maturing faster than she had hoped. Still, she wasn't going to try to force him to believe in something that he had clearly outgrown.

"Well, just remember that Louise and Georgie still believe in Santa, so don't spoil it for them, OK?" his mother asked. "Besides, even if you are Mister Smarty Pants All Grown Up, you're still my little boy and you could pretend for me too."

"OK, Mom," James said.

He wondered just how long his mother would consider him to be her little boy.

Lorraine reminded James about bath time, and

went back downstairs to clean up after dinner. When she got there, she discovered that it had already been taken care of.

"Thanks Doris," she said to her aunt who was preparing a cup of tea.

"Believe it or not, it wasn't me," Doris replied. Charles shooed me out of here and took care of it all. I was tempted to check his forehead to see if he had a fever."

"Maybe he's trying to get on Santa's good side," Lorraine suggested with a wink.

She decided to go and find out just what Charles had in mind that he'd like to find under the Christmas tree this year. She walked into the living room and stopped short.

"Oh no!" she gasped.

"What is it," Charles asked, thinking some great calamity had befallen the household.

"The tree," she exclaimed. "We didn't buy a Christmas tree."

"I completely forgot about it," said Charles. "O'Reilly won't be there tomorrow, so we'll have to wait a day or two. If we pick it up then, well still have it decorated in lots of time for Christmas. I'll bring the decorations upstairs tomorrow and we can put some of the things around, we just won't have a tree for a few more days."

"We can't do it tomorrow night, because we have to go to the school for parent-teacher night," Lorraine said. "But, let's not say anything to the children about it. If they notice we'll tell them that we aren't sure whether to have a tree this year, then it will be a surprise for them when it comes on Tuesday."

Charles returned to his newspaper, and Lorraine sat down beside him. While she liked having the tree up, she was happy in a way that they didn't have it yet. She was tired from all of the baking she had done earlier in the day, and with the frantic pace of activities that had gone on in the previous few days, a quiet evening watching television was a welcome diversion.

Just as James had done earlier in the day, it wasn't long before she dozed off in the warm living room. Charles was just a few minutes behind her. Neither of them heard James slip past the living room door in a quest to liberate a few cookies from the kitchen.

Chapter Ten

Decorations But Missing A Tree

James woke up early on Sunday morning, dressed and slipped quietly downstairs. He slid his feet into the new galoshes, put on his coat and headed out the door to see how the skating rink looked.

The sun barely had risen over the southeast horizon, but it reflected off the fresh ice of the rink in a brilliant prism of color. James would have liked to test the ice by sliding across its surface, but he remembered his father saying that it would need more coats of water before it would be ready for use.

He thought about taking the saucer to River Ravine Park, but the memory of his inglorious decent down the Hill Of The Seven Bumps was still fresh in his mind, and even fresher on his backside. He decided he would wait a few days – or weeks - before attempting another run. Besides, the saucer was pretty dented and mangled after the last run and he wasn't sure how well or if it would even go down the hill.

He heard a church bell tolling in the distance and remembered that it was Sunday. He wasn't a big fan of Sunday mornings. He would have to put on his good clothes and accompany Aunt Doris and his sister and brother to church at eleven o'clock. While Doris went into the main church, the children would be hustled off to the basement for Sunday school classes.

James' Sunday school class was taught by a woman who appeared to be about ten years older than Doris was. She seemed to think it was her place to put the fear of God into her charges, telling them about the many things she considered evil in the world. She reminded James of his Aunt Millicent, as she lectured the group of ten-year-olds about alcohol, tobacco and television. She was particularly against anything that made Christmas seem like a fun time for children. As far as she was concerned, the world would be better off if there was no element of the holiday that did not concern itself with the birth of Jesus. Christmas gifts, decorations, and holiday spirit were works of the devil.

"It's no coincidence that Santa and Satan use the

exact same letters in their names," she would say.

On a bright sunny winter morning just four days before Christmas, the last place James wanted to go was to Sunday school. It didn't seem fair to James that his sister spent the hour coloring pictures from bible stories, while he had to listen to old Miss Watson rant.

Charles was the sort of man who attended church twice a year; once at Christmas and again at Easter. Beyond that, his role in the religious upbringing of the children was limited to driving them and his wife's aunt to the church and picking them up again when it was finished.

Lorraine enjoyed church, but given the choice between having some quiet time alone at home and listening to the octogenarian minister repeat virtually the same sermon he gave every week, she opted for the time alone. She was sure that God understood.

James heard the back door open. He turned and saw his father coming out to join him in the back yard.

"You mean you've been out here all this time and you haven't brought the hose out yet?" his father called. "Come on and give me a hand.

James ran to his father's side and they walked to the garage.

"I'll connect the water to the tap and you drag the hose out to the rink," his father said with a smile. "We want to give the ice a good chance to freeze, don't we?"

James dragged the hose out through the garage door, and pulled it to the edge of the rink. He ran back to join his father.

"I'll go out and get the nozzle set and you turn the water on when I call," Charles instructed.

As soon as he heard his father shout, he turned on the tap and ran back outside. Charles was standing at the edge of the rink with the hose in his hand, but no water was coming through the nozzle. Despite draining it carefully, some water had obviously frozen inside the hose overnight creating a blockage.

Charles turned the nozzle on and off several times and shook the hose. Without thinking, he looked at the end of the nozzle and turned in on, just as the blockage cleared. Cold water shot through the nozzle and hit Charles straight in the face, blowing his hat from his head.

"Damnation!" he shouted.

It was one of the words he reserved for the most serious annoyances in his life. Getting his faced washed with water barely warmer than the freezing point certainly qualified.

James stood spellbound. He had a very strong urge to laugh at the sight of his father's calamity, but he knew that it would not be wise to do so. He chose instead to remain motionless, in the hopes that it would make him appear invisible.

Charles turned and saw his son. The boy was staring at him with his jaw dropped. He realized that he probably would have laughed if he saw the same thing happen to someone else and chuckled to himself.

"I guess that wasn't a good word to use to wake up the neighborhood on a Sunday morning," Charles said.

That shocked James even more. His father had never shown any ability or desire to laugh at his own calamities before. His sudden change from the cursing soaking wet father to the laughing soaking wet father was very odd.

"You OK, Dad?" James finally asked.

"Oh, I'll live," Charles replied. "It sure woke me up, though."

Charles started hosing down the surface of the skating rink. For the next ten minutes he added water until he had a pool about two inches deep spread across the whole area.

When he was done, he said to James, "Let's drain the hose and bring it inside the house this time. That will prevent it from freezing and giving me a cold shower again. But let's do it quickly, before I freeze to death."

Charles took the hose down to the basement, while James went into the kitchen. His mother was cooking eggs for breakfast and the aromas and warmth of the kitchen were very inviting.

Charles went upstairs after putting the hose away and dried his wet cold hair. When he returned to the kitchen, he sat down at the table and took a long drink from his coffee cup, letting the hot liquid thaw his insides.

"After breakfast I need you to help me downstairs, James," Charles said.

"But don't I have to go to Sunday school today?" James asked hoping his father would grant him a reprieve.

"Hmmm, I guess you're right, James," Charles said. "I'm sure you'd much rather spend an hour listening to Miss Watson than help me downstairs."

"No. That's OK," James said quickly.

While Charles drove Doris, Louise and Georgie to the church, James sat at the kitchen table with his mother, who was drinking her coffee and working on the crossword puzzle in the newspaper.

"Dad seems different," James said.

"Better or worse?" Lorraine asked.

"Well, better I guess," the boy replied. "It's just that he seems like he's trying to be more fun than he used to."

"Then it's a good thing, James. Just go with the flow. Everything will be fine," she said. She wasn't entirely sure if she was trying to convince her son or herself.

Charles was indeed acting differently, but he had tried to explain it to her over coffee the day before, and it seemed like he was sincere about the changes he wanted to make. She was happy to have him more involved in the family.

When Charles returned, he sat and had another cup of coffee before he and James descended the stairs into the basement.

The basement was dark and windowless. A couple of light bulbs hung from the ceiling. In one corner, there was the wringer washing machine and a large laundry basin. There were also a couple of large racks for drying clothes in the winter. Along another wall sat Charles' tools and a workbench. The furnace banged and rattled in the opposite corner, near the small room where coal had been stored before the furnace was converted to oil burning. That room was now filled with boxes. Somewhere in the pile were the ones containing the family's Christmas decorations.

Charles passed boxes to James and the boy restacked them in the main part of the basement.

"Why are we getting out the decorations, Dad? We don't even have a tree to put them on," James asked.

"Well, were going to put a few decorations up in the living room and in the hall," his father replied.

It worried James. He tended to worry when things weren't following the order he expected them to. Certainly, this Christmas was quite out of order. They always had their Christmas tree up and decorated by now. He decided that the purchase of the new car had not only meant that he'd be hearing that it was a gift for the whole family, but that it had also left too little money for his parents to buy a tree.

James and Charles carried the boxes of decorations up to the living room, where Lorraine waited to start unpacking them. When all the boxes had made their way upstairs, Charles and James returned to the basement to put the other boxes back into the storage room. When that chore was completed, Charles looked around the room, seemingly trying to size it up.

"You, know, James," he said, "We've got a fair bit of room down here. Maybe we could straighten up the rest of the basement and then there'd be room for something else."

"Like what?" James asked.

"Oh, I don't know. Maybe I could make a bigger

workbench, or get some more tools," Charles suggested.

That thought didn't do much for James. He was not overly interested in the tools his father already had set up in the basement, and viewed them as potential weapons of self-destruction. He was convinced that it would be easier to cut a straight line through his fingers with his father's table saw, than it would be to use it to cut a straight line through a piece of wood.

By the time they were finished, they had opened a space that could easily hold a sheet of plywood mounted on two sawhorses with a couple of stools around the outside of the board. James had no idea that was exactly what would be going there.

When Charles and James returned to the living room, Lorraine was surrounded by partially empty boxes of Christmas decorations.

A nativity scene was displayed on a small table in the corner. It was a wooden stable containing miniature people, cows, sheep, donkeys and camels. Over the top, hanging from the ceiling with a piece of fishing line was Harold the angel. James had given him that name when he was four or five years old, because he assumed he was the Harold angel that everyone made everyone stop and say "Hark! It's Harold the Angel singing."

A plastic wreath was hanging over the mirror

above the mantel. The photographs that normally lined the mantelpiece had been taken down and replaced with red and green candles, a Santa figurine, and a tiny church with a light bulb shining inside it to illuminate the tiny stained glass windows along the side. It had a key in the back that when wound ran a music box that played Oh Come All Ye Faithful.

In the front window, as always, was the small electric menorah that Lorraine placed there each year "out of respect for the neighbors."

A large green felt Christmas tree hung from the hook in the wall that normally held the photograph of Charles' mother sternly looking out over the room. Lorraine was busy attaching the Christmas cards they had already received to the felt. By the time the holidays ended, the tree would be filled to capacity with brightly colored cards.

"Oh, James," Lorraine said as he entered the room. "You're just in time to help me repack all the decorations for the tree that I had to take out of the boxes to get to the ones I needed."

"So it's true then," James thought. "We aren't going to have a tree this year. That car must have taken all the money Mom and Dad have."

James didn't say anything to his mother about the lack of a tree or his feelings about it. He helped her repack the boxes and carried them to the place under the stairs where they were stored during the holidays.

Christmas carols were playing on the radio. The unmistakable sound of Nat King Cole's voice filled the room as he sang the opening lines of a song.

"Chestnuts roasting on an open fire…"

"I just love that song," Lorraine said as she hummed along with the tune. "There's just something Christmassy about the thought of hot roasted chestnuts. I wish we could do it here."

"It might be a little difficult," Charles said. "Something about the lack of an open fire to roast them on."

"Oh I know," Lorraine said. "Still…"

The Kelly living room did feature a large fireplace with the heavy wooden mantelpiece that was now adorned with Christmas decorations. The hearth had long ago been sealed. In its place, a small electric device gave the appearance of flames. The light bulb inside it wasn't likely to produce enough heat to roast a chestnut.

Still, the thought planted a seed in Charles' brain. He would find a way to get roasted chestnuts for Lorraine in time for Christmas.

James decided to go outside for a while. He checked on the progress of the skating rink. A thin sheet of ice now covered the water that he and his father had added earlier in the day, but he could still see the unfrozen water moving in between the main surface and the new ice. It would be a while longer before it was ready for the final application.

He decided to see what Coop was doing. James walked around to the front of the house and down the driveway to the sidewalk. A huge pile of snow marked the front corner of every driveway all the way along Parkland Road, thanks to the efforts of Steve Murphy and his snowplow. As winter wore on the piles would only become higher, but the boys made good use of them. They became the forts they defended in prolonged snowball wars throughout the season.

When James got to the front of the Cooper house, he could see into their living room. The whole family was working on decorating a huge Christmas tree that filled the front window. It only stood to remind James about their treeless living room. He decided to go back to his own yard and start working on his snowball collection. He'd need a good supply to properly defend Fort Kelly from attackers. He also needed a secret stash of snowballs that would be aimed at a certain younger sister, when the right opportunity arose. He didn't expect that opportunity to come so fast.

He looked down the street and saw an imposing figure walking determinedly towards him, trailed by two children. As they got closer he could see that it was his Aunt Doris with Louise and Georgie tagging along behind.

Aunt Doris did not look pleased. Charles had forgotten to go back to the church to pick them up.

James took one of the better snowballs and ran behind the garage. This would be his opportunity to retaliate for Louise's surprise snowball attack on him on that first snowy day.

He waited until he heard them approaching the side door. In one quick movement, he stepped from behind the garage and launched the snowball. It would have been a perfect sneak attack had the snowball not stuck to the wool fibers on his mitten for a moment longer than he anticipated. It took a slightly different trajectory than he had planned. Instead of a direct path to the back of his sister's head, the snowball arced several feet into the air and as it started his descent, anyone could have seen what was going to happen. He probably should have shouted a warning, but there was no time really, and the shock of what was about to happen left him speechless.

Just as Doris placed her hand on the doorknob, fully prepared to give Charles a piece of her mind for forgetting to come and pick her and the children up at church, the snowball found its mark. It hit her slightly above and behind her left ear and quickly disintegrated sending icy shrapnel cascading down inside her coat.

Doris forgot about being angry with Charles as she spun on her heals. James stood frozen in the same spot he had occupied since firing the snowball. He quickly looked up at the eave, hoping that Doris might think it was simply a lump of snow that had fallen from the roof.

Doris' cheeks were already red from the long walk in the cold combined with her anger about being left at the church. The snowy greeting she had just gotten from her great-nephew only served to enhance the color in her face. Her eyes squinted and a small artery pulsed at the edge of her forehead. James couldn't ever recall seeing her look like that and it scared him.

Between clenched teeth, Doris managed to say, "James, I think you'd better come inside now."

She turned and opened the door. Louise knew the snowball had been aimed at her and she stuck her tongue out a James just before going in. When the door closed behind them James was still standing in the same spot mentally tracing the trajectory of his snowball, trying to determine what had made it go so terribly wrong.

He was still there when the door reopened. His mother was standing on the stoop, with her arms folded. That was never a good sign.

"James Albert Kelly…" she said, letting her voice carry throughout the neighborhood. The use of his full name was always an indication that he was in more than a little trouble.

James still stood in the same spot, trying hard to come up with some sort of an explanation as to why he had just given his great-aunt a soaker snowball right behind the ear and down her coat.

"Do you have anything to say for yourself?" his mother asked.

"It was an accident," James started to say, drawing back on an excuse that had served him well when he was much younger.

"So you're telling me that a snowball accidentally shot from your hand and hit Aunt Doris behind the ear?" his mother questioned.

"Well, it was supposed to hit Louise," he protested.

"Ah, I see. You were trying to hit your younger sister," she stated.

James knew as soon as he said it that it was no better to hit his sister than it was to hit his aunt. It had been drilled into him that good boys did not hit girls, although he was sure that his mother wouldn't protest too much if his Aunt Millicent had been accidentally smacked with a soaker snowball.

"But Louise hit me with a snowball the other day, and it was the first snowball of the season and I was really mad, and Aunt Doris and Georgie were in the window laughing at me and..." James protested, trying to fit as many excuses for throwing the snowball into a single sentence as he could. "It just isn't fair. If she can throw one at me, I should be able to throw one at her."

James was almost on the verge of tears. He was mad at the unfairness of the rules. He was upset that it looked like there would be no Christmas tree in the Kelly house this year. He was even miffed that the snowball hadn't hit his sister, because that meant that she was a better aim than he was.

"Well, James, you'd better march right in here and apologize to Aunt Doris," his mother demanded. "After that you can go and think about it in your room for a while."

James walked dejectedly into the house and took off his coat and galoshes. As he passed the living room on his way to his aunt's room, he saw his father. When their eyes met, Charles quickly looked the other way and cleared his throat. He didn't want his son to get the idea that he thought the whole idea of Doris being smacked by a snowball was funny. He knew if he accidentally started to laugh, he would be in almost as much trouble as his son was at that moment.

James went to his aunt's door and tentatively knocked on it.

"Yes," Doris answered.

The boy opened the door and stepped into the room. Doris was sitting in her rocking chair knitting. She had a towel wrapped around her wet hair like a turban.

"I'm sorry," James started trying hard to keep the tears of embarrassment from flowing down his cheeks. "I wasn't aiming for you."

"Well, you certainly got me, didn't you," Doris said trying to sound stern, but failing as she broke into a laugh. "It must have been quite a sight, you throwing the snowball and realizing that it wasn't going to hit your intended target, and me getting walloped in the side of the head with it."

James smiled for the first time since the snowball had left his hand.

"I don't know," he said. "When I saw what was going to happen I closed my eyes."

Lorraine came into the room when she heard the two of them laughing.

"Has this boy apologized?" she asked.

"Yes, he did," said Doris, "But he'd just better watch his step in the future. I may be old, but I think I can probably still throw a snowball pretty well."

On hearing the laughter, Charles decided it might be safe for him to come to Doris' room and apologize for forgetting to pick her up.

"I guess I got caught up in my work, Doris," he said. "You should have gone over to the rectory and called home."

"Oh," the older woman said. "So it's my fault that I walked all the way home is it?"

"Well, no, I mean," Charles stammered.

He looked at James who seemed to be enjoying seeing his father squirm and remembered his son's typical excuse.

"It was an accident," he said.

The Kelly's had been one of the last families on Parkland Drive to get a television set. A few months after Charles' mother had died, Georgie came along. While Lorraine was in the hospital giving birth, Charles brought home a television set to keep the older children occupied. James and Louise always credited their younger brother with the arrival of TV in their home, even if they did use it to terrify him with the clown on Big Top Circus.

After dinner was finished, the family sat in the living room waiting for the Sunday night special showing of It's A Wonderful Life. Georgie was already in bed, and the older children were in their pajamas ready to head to bed as soon as the movie was over.

George Bailey faced the dilemma of the missing money from the Savings and Loan. He told Mr. Potter that he had a life insurance policy worth $500.00, and failing to get the old man's help decided to commit suicide.

James suddenly remembered his father's telephone call that he had listened to a couple of days earlier. He started to think about how differently his father was acting, and that he was borrowing money because of something that had happened at work. It didn't take the boy too long to put two and two together and come up with five. He was convinced that his father, like George Bailey, was contemplating suicide.

James looked at his father, who was intently watching the movie. While Charles was just enjoying the film, James saw his keen interest in it to be another sign that he was contemplating following George Bailey's lead.

James got up and went upstairs to his room. He lay on his bed wondering what he could do to prevent his father from doing what he was obviously planning. The events of the past few days went through his mind, all adding up to the same misconception. His father was acting differently. He didn't care if the lawn got ruined by a skating rink anymore. He went out and got a new car to make sure the family had reliable transportation after he was gone. He lied to him about Christmas shopping. He had stopped going to work. He didn't even care if there was a Christmas tree or not, probably because he wasn't going to be here to take it down after Christmas.

Chapter Eleven

An Embarrassment of Trees

Life returned pretty much to normal after the weekend. As normal, that is, as life can be with just two days left in the school term and four days to go until Christmas.

James and his father put the finishing touches on the skating rink after dinner on Monday night. The final layer was the most difficult, because it required that they bring pails of hot water out to the rink from the kitchen. The hot water melted away the cracks in the ice and gave the Kelly Forum a smooth skating surface.

It was difficult to concentrate on schoolwork during the day. He found himself daydreaming about skating and the Christmas holiday several times each day. Luckily, he was always able to snap out of it before Miss Witherspoon asked him a question. The last thing he wanted was to face another detention this close to the vacation.

Class time was spent mainly going over the tests from the previous week. James had passed all of them with marks high enough that he knew his parents would be pleased. Coop's papers all seemed to have the bright pink slips attached to them that meant he was going to have to get his parents to sign them to let Miss Witherspoon know that they were aware of just how poorly their son was doing.

The remainder of the school day was once again dedicated to art. The children continued to make decorations for their trees at home. Irv and Sadie were allowed to make artificial menorahs using the toilet paper tubes left over from the star construction the previous week. James thought that maybe he should ask if he could do the same because it was painfully clear that there was not going to be a tree in the Kelly house to hold his paper decorations.

As the day went on, the paper bag mailboxes the children had made started to fill with cards. At Christmastime there wasn't the stigma attached to dropping a card into a girl's bag that there was when it came time for Valentine's Day cards. Everyone knew that it was just a given that boys would wish girls a Merry Christmas and girls would pass the same sentiment on to them. In general, every boy and girl got a card from every other classmate at

Christmas. Most of the children tried to set aside the ones that said Happy Holidays or some other similar generic statement for the cards that they'd tuck into Irv and Sadie's bags. James' mother made a special trip to the store so that he could give them each a card wishing a Happy Hanukah.

Late in the afternoon, Miss Witherspoon called the children to attention. Each child had been given an assignment to bring some form of cookies or similar items to school the next day and she didn't want any of them to forget.

"Now class," she said, "I know that some of your parents are having a hard time with expenses this year. We've all enjoyed our class Christmas tree and it would be a shame to see it go to waste. If any of your families aren't going to be able to have a Christmas tree this year, leave a note for me on my desk tomorrow morning and I will be sure to pick a deserving family to get our tree."

"That's it!" thought James. "I can ask Miss Witherspoon for the class tree and then we'll be able to have one. Mom and Dad will be so surprised and I'll bet they'll be really thankful."

When James got home that afternoon, he didn't go out to the skating rink. He rushed to his bedroom to prepare a note that Miss Witherspoon would be sure to pick him for the Christmas tree donation.

In his best penmanship he wrote, "Dear Miss Witherspoon: My father had to buy a new car last week and it has taken all the money we have, so we won't be having a Christmas tree this year. I know my sister and little brother are going to be really sad if we don't have a tree for Christmas morning, even though the car is going to have to be the gift for the whole family. I would really like it if you could give me the class tree. Yours truly, James Kelly."

James slipped downstairs and asked his mother for one of her special Christmas cards for Miss Witherspoon.

"What happened to the one for your teacher in your package," she asked.

"Oh, I gave it to her," James replied knowing that he was going to have to think up an excuse for giving her another card if he wanted his Christmas tree plan to remain secret. "It's just that she got a whole lot of the exact same cards, and I was thinking it would be nice to give her a special one."

"Well, that's very thoughtful of you James," his mother said, proud of her son who she thought was finally showing some maturity in the way he felt about his teacher.

James returned to his room with the card, and a couple of Christmas cookies his mother had given him "just for being nice to Miss Witherspoon." He signed it and neatly folded his note, placing it in the envelope. On the envelope he wrote, "For Miss Witherspoon. Urgent Christmas message enclosed."

The next day, he casually slipped the envelope onto Miss Witherspoon's desk. All morning long it sat there, while the teacher read the class Christmas stories from books she had taken out of the library. As time slipped by, James was getting worried that she might not have seen the note. When he came back in after recess, he moved the note into the middle of her desk so she couldn't possibly miss it.

Finally, just before noon, James saw Miss Witherspoon pick up the envelope. She was about to open it when Mr. Armstrong, the school principal came into the room. Miss Witherspoon set James' envelope back down on her desk and walked to the door to speak to the principal.

As he was leaving, he turned and wished the class a merry Christmas and a happy Hanukah to Irv and Sadie. Through the entire time, James had never taken his gaze off the envelope. The bell rang for lunch before Miss Witherspoon had a chance to get back to it.

All through lunch, James worried about whether his teacher would read his note. He became even more worried when he saw that it was still sitting on her desk when he returned for the afternoon. Once again, he centered it on her desk.

The room was filled with children laughing and excitedly opening the Christmas cards that had been deposited in their bags. Two folding tables had been set up across the back of the room and each child piled their donation to the party on top of it. There were sugar cookies, mincemeat tarts, gingerbread men, and a huge bowl of Christmas candies.

James was too worried to think about the goodies. He just wanted Miss Witherspoon to read his note. Hadn't she seen that he had marked the envelope with the word urgent?

Finally, while the children were busy opening the bags of Christmas cards, the teacher picked up James note and opened it. She smiled at the picture on the front of the card. As she opened it, James' note fell out landing under her desk. For a moment, while she read the inside of the card, James thought she hadn't noticed his letter falling from the card. Finally, she set the card on her desk and reached under it to retrieve the note. She opened it and read the words James had so carefully written.

"Oh the poor boy," she thought as she read the note remembering the two days after the arrival of the snow that James had to come to school without galoshes.

She closed the note and slipped it into her purse. It gave her a chance to compose herself from the sadness she felt for the Kelly family. She hadn't realized that they were in such dire straits. They hadn't mentioned anything the previous night at parent-teacher night, but she assumed that was just their attempt to maintain some degree of pride. Finally, she looked up and caught James' eye. She smiled at him and gave him a little nod. Both knew that she was saying that there would indeed be a Christmas tree at the Kelly house this year.

James raced home after school. He wanted to be sure and be there when the tree was delivered. He anticipated just how thrilled his mother was going to be that he had managed to get them their very own Christmas tree, despite all the money that had gone into buying a new car.

Shortly after four o'clock, the doorbell rang. James went to his spot at the top of the stairs so he could hear his mother's reaction.

Lorraine turned to Doris in the kitchen and said, "Well we know that won't be Millicent because she just barges in after ringing the bell."

James heard his mother open the door. There were voices outside on the front porch. He knew that one of them belonged to his teacher, and the other sounded like the school janitor, Mac Roney. He wasn't prepared to hear his mother protesting the arrival of the tree.

"Oh no! No! No! No!" Lorraine said. "There has to be a misunderstanding."

James slipped down the stairs to see what was going on. His mother had invited Miss Witherspoon and Mr. Roney in, and she was trying to explain to them that they did indeed have plans to get a tree that very evening. There had been a delay in getting it and they planned to surprise the children with it. James just thought that there wasn't going to be a tree.

"Now, Mrs. Kelly,: Miss Witherspoon said. "Don't let your pride get in the way. James has done a very grown up thing asking for the class tree to help you through this financial crisis."

"But we're not in a financial crisis," Lorraine exclaimed. "We just haven't bought our tree yet. Charles left a half hour ago to go and get one."

Lorraine started to cry, partly out of embarrassment that her son's teacher thought that they were poor, and partially out of sadness that her son also thought that the family was too poor to buy a Christmas tree.

Miss Witherspoon put her hand on Loraine's shoulder, "There, there, Mrs. Kelly. We all go through these things at some point in our lives. I'm just glad we were able to help you with this small gesture. Mr. Roney and I will see ourselves out. You just do your very best to have a Merry Christmas and we'll all hope the New Year brings better times for you."

After the door closed, Doris came into the living room.

"What was that all about?" she asked.

"Oh, Doris," Lorraine sobbed. "They thought we were too poor to buy a Christmas tree. James must have told his teacher that we weren't going to have a tree this year. It was all going to be a surprise for the children when Charles brings one home tonight. I'm so embarrassed."

Doris started to laugh. She sat down on the couch because she knew that this was going to be one of those times that if she let the laughter fully escape it was going to take her breath away.

"Oh for the love of Pete," she said. "I haven't heard anything that funny since Charles called and said he'd been arrested."

James realized that, despite his best intentions, his plan had backfired rather spectacularly. He quietly slipped back up the stairs and into his bedroom. He felt badly because he knew his mother was crying because of what he had done. He also knew that Aunt Doris was laughing at the whole situation. Neither reaction made him feel very good.

This had to be the worst Christmas ever.

An hour later, Charles pulled in the driveway. He had stopped at Pat O'Rielly's Christmas tree lot and picked out a large pine tree. The new Squire was perfect for toting home a tree of that size. It fit neatly along the roof between the two racks making it easy to tie down. He was pleased with the tree and pleased with the car. He was also pleased with himself for successfully trying to make some changes in the way he lived his life.

This had to be the best Christmas ever.

Charles pulled in the driveway without looking at the front of the house. If he had, he would have noticed that there already was a Christmas tree waiting on the porch. He untied the tree from the roof of the station wagon, and hauled it around to the front of the house. He stopped to catch his breath at the bottom of the steps and decided that the best way to bring a tree of that size into the house was to pull it backwards up the steps. As he reached the top step and was about to pull the tree the last way up, he felt some resistance behind him. He turned to see what was blocking his way and found that he had neatly surrounded himself with evergreens.

"Where the Sam Hill did this come from," he shouted to no one in particular.

No one ever knew who or where Sam Hill was, but it was an expression that Charles had picked up somewhere. He used it whenever things weren't quite bad enough for him to use 'damnation.'

He knew that there had definitely not been a tree there when he left earlier and he could not figure out how his wife had managed to get one there herself. Leaving his tree behind, he walked into the house.

"Lorraine," he called. "What's a Christmas tree doing already on the front porch?"

Lorraine came into the front hall from the living room. Charles could tell that she was upset, but the sound of Doris's laughter made it seem like things were slightly off kilter around the house.

"Oh Charles," she said, barely able to hold back

her tears. "I'm so embarrassed. James told his teacher that we were too poor to afford a Christmas tree this year, so she had the janitor deliver the class tree to us."

Charles stared at his wife in disbelief. He looked at Doris who was wiping tears from her eyes, but it was clear that her tears had nothing to do with embarrassment or sadness. The old woman could barely contain her laughter.

"Where on Earth would he get an idea like that?" Charles asked.

"I don't know," Lorraine sobbed. "I've been too upset to go and ask him and he's been hiding in his room ever since he saw my reaction to them delivering the tree. I tried to explain it to them, but that teacher just wouldn't listen. She's convinced we're just a step away from the poorhouse."

Charles took off his coat and hung it up in the hall. He climbed the stairs and went into James' room. The boy was lying on the bed with his back to the door.

"So, what do you know about this tree situation, Son?" he asked.

James turned to look at his father. He, too, had obviously been crying.

"I was just trying to help, Dad," he said, his voice choked on his own embarrassment and sadness. "We didn't have a tree, and you had to spend all that money on a new car last week, so I figured we couldn't afford one this year. I know how much Mom likes having a tree and I didn't want her, Louise, or Georgie to have to do without one."

"James," Charles said, starting to see why Doris

thought the whole mess was so funny. "With everything that was going on last weekend your mother and I just forgot to go out and buy a tree, so we thought we'd wait until tonight and surprise you. I've got a great big pine outside on the porch that I could use your help with before dinner."

James wiped his eyes.

"I'm really sorry I made Mom so upset," he said.

"Oh I think she'll get over it," Charles said with a grin. "It'll probably end up being one of those stories that gets told every Christmas."

Charles went back downstairs and explained the misunderstanding to his wife and her aunt. By the time he was finished, even Lorraine could see the humor in the situation. She went to the kitchen, took two gingerbread men from the cookie tin, and carried them upstairs.

"James," she called as she entered his room. "I think what you did was very nice. I'm sorry we made you worry about whether or not we could afford a tree. It was your father's and my fault that we just plain forgot to buy one last weekend."

Mother and son sat on the edge of the boy's bed and ate the cookies.

"You know," she said between mouthfuls, "I think that, in the end, this is going to be our best Christmas ever."

James was still not entirely sure.

The doorbell rang again. Lorraine looked at

James, briefly worrying about what else might be in store to embarrass her. She was relieved when the look on James face told her that he had no other surprises arranged.

Charles opened the door to Mary Cooper, who had a handwritten flyer she was delivering throughout the neighborhood.

Skating Lessons For Children

Call Mary Cooper

555-8936

Mary had been taking figure skating lessons ever since she was four years old. She had made a bit of a name for herself in town after she won the junior city championship the previous winter. That gave her an automatic berth in this year's state championships. Mike had told Charles that despite being very proud of his daughter's prowess on the ice, the expense was extremely high.

"Her skates alone cost me what I make on the profit of a new car down at the dealership," he had said.

"I'm trying to earn some extra money over the Christmas vacation," she told Charles. "I'm hoping to earn enough to pay for a new skating costume that I saw and would really like to wear at the state championships. We have our skating rink in the backyard and I am teaching beginners to skate and some of the younger girls in the neighborhood some simple figure skating techniques."

Lorraine and James had come downstairs in time to hear Mary's business proposal.

"That would be great for Louise and Georgie," James said.

"You meant that would be great for James because Louise and Georgie would be skating on the Cooper's rink instead of ours," his father corrected.

James blushed. That was his exact thought. He just didn't think it would be quite that obvious.

When Mary left, having signed up both of the younger Kelly children for her skating lessons, Charles turned to James and said, "OK, Kiddo. You can work off their lessons by giving me a hand with this tree."

Putting a tree in the stand was probably the worst part of the entire holiday season for Charles. No matter how straight a tree looked on O'Reilly's lot, it always seemed to lose that quality on the drive home.

Fitting the tree into the stand was the first problem. The trunk was always too big to fit into the ring. It meant a lot of sawing, shaving, and good measure of cursing was required to get the tree standing.

"One of these years I'm going to cut a hole in the floor and fill it with wet concrete to stick the tree into," Charles said. "That'd hold it better than this cockamamie Christmas tree stand." By the time they were finished, both James and his father had pinesap sticking to their hands and on their faces where they had wiped away the perspiration the effort produced. Pine needles were intertwined into their hair, giving them an elflike appearance.

James and Charles retrieved the boxes from under the stairs just before Doris called them to the dining room for dinner. Doris took one look at them when they walked into the room and started laughing.

"You two look like you've been in the midst of a serious lumberjacking disaster," she said pointing at the mirror that hung over the china cabinet.

James and Charles followed her finger and saw themselves in the mirror. Both started to smile at their appearance.

"Like father, like son." Charles chortled. James liked that.

"You're not going to come to this table looking like that," the old woman admonished. "I've worked hard on dinner and don't want my appetite spoiled by looking at the two of you filthy beings."

James and Charles turned and headed upstairs to the bathroom to try to clean up before returning to the table. Neither of them was willing to argue with Doris. It took the better part of half an hour to make themselves look presentable. James face was bright red from scouring off the sticky pine gum with the strong red soap his father preferred.

When they got back downstairs, Lorraine was in the living room looking at the tree trying to decide which was its best side.

Doris called from the dining room, "If we don't sit down and eat this dinner, it's going to be as dry as peat."

"So, pretty much the same as usual," Charles commented.

"I'll pretend I didn't hear that," Doris replied.

The two of them had kept up this constant banter for as long as James could remember. To an outsider it might seem like they were antagonistic. Everyone in the Kelly household knew that the two had a deep affection for one another. In many ways, Charles wished his mother could have been more like Doris.

Dinner was indeed overcooked. The meatloaf had a thick dry crust around the edges and the peas, something that was normally cooked to the point that no flavor remained, were so wizened and mushy that they were barely recognizable.

It was one of those meals that made James thankful to whoever it was that invented ketchup.

After dinner, Charles started stringing the lights around the tree. James particularly liked the ones that looked like small candles filled with liquid. When they were lit, the liquid bubbled inside the clear tubes.

Lorraine took care of most of the ornaments, taking special care to place the oldest ones in the most predominant places on the tree. When she was finished, the children added the decorations that they had made at school. Georgie squealed with delight as every new ornament was added. He was too young to have remembered previous Christmases.

The finale was the addition of the foil icicles. Lorraine produced a package of icicles that she had carefully saved and wrapped in waxed paper from previous years. She did not believe in wasting anything, not even used tinsel.

Lorraine turned off the lamps in the living room so that the only light was coming from the tree. It was a beautiful sight. Even Georgie sat in silence and stared at it. James and Louise sat on the couch and watched the light dance off the tinsel. Lorraine put her arm around Charles' waist.

"It's the best tree we've ever had," she said, resting her head against his arm.

"You say that every year," he said.

"Yes, but this time I really mean it," she replied giving him a squeeze.

"When do we put up our stockings?" Louise asked.

"Not until Christmas Eve silly," James said. "It's tradition or something."

Lorraine took Georgie upstairs to get him ready for bed. Doris called Louise to help her roll a skein of wool into a ball, leaving Charles and James alone in the living room.

"So did you have Christmas trees like this when you were my age, Dad?" James said.

"Well, do you mean back when the dinosaurs roamed the Earth?" Charles replied.

"No, Dad," James said. "When you were a kid and your aunts gave you a train set."

"Oh, then," Charles said, pretending not to notice the heavy hint his son was making by bringing up the subject of trains. "Well, my mother didn't care much about Christmas or toys, James. You could say she was a bit of a Scrooge. I guess that's where I got the idea ingrained in me that Christmas was a time for things you need, not necessarily for things you want."

Charles felt badly when he realized that he was so much like his mother. He remembered friends who got the things he would have liked to receive, and he remembered what it felt like to see them with their new toys or sports equipment.

"It's something about that generation, James, and mine too for that matter. Times were pretty tough for a lot of people during the Depression and they remember that, so spending money on something frivolous just wasn't a priority."

Charles tussled the boy's hair and added, "Why don't you sneak into the kitchen and see if you can slip a couple of gingerbread cookies out of their hiding place."

When the boy had gone, Charles looked at the tree. He thought about how his mother had dictated the way he had treated the holidays, and for that matter how Doris was continuing to do so now. He made an early New Year's resolution that that was all about to change.

This year was going to be a little different. He was actually looking forward to the holiday. He was especially anxious to see James' reaction to the electric train set. It was all he could do to keep from spilling the secret before Christmas morning.

Chapter Twelve

The Eve of Anticipation

Christmas Eve brought with it a light snowfall. Charles reminded James to clear the driveway and the sidewalk, and to clear the skating rink, as well.

"Maybe when I get home we can shoot the puck around together," he said.

That surprised James, but the boy was getting used to feeling surprised by his father lately. He had never shown much interest in playing sports. The only time he had tried to help James prepare for Little League baseball, the ball had sailed through the master bedroom window, ending the practice once and for all.

Charles headed downtown to Christmas shop for Lorraine's gift. He had always fallen prey to the perfume counter in previous years, even though he hated the smell of the stuff and it tended to make his sinuses close.

This year he finally took note of Lorraine's table in the bedroom. Neatly arranged across the back was a line of perfume bottles, representing several Christmases past. Most of them had never been opened. He wondered why he had never realized that his wife didn't like the stuff either, but summed it up to the fact that she always seemed so pleased to receive it.

Lorraine was pleased to receive anything from Charles. She loved him deeply, but she knew he was just not the shopping kind of husband. Many years she had gone shopping for a Christmas present for herself and then suggested that Charles wrap it up for her "for the sake of the children." Those gifts were usually some sort of clothing like the new winter coat she had bought for him to wrap up this year.

Charles knew that she would be expecting to unwrap the coat and a bottle of perfume, and that she'd be perfectly happy to do so, but since he was making changes to the way he was treating the children this Christmas, he wanted the same for his wife.

After an hour of looking at and then rejecting a wide variety of possible gifts for Lorraine, Charles finally settled on a delicate watch.

As he walked back to the car, he passed a small fruit stand. In front of the store there was a large bin filled to overflowing with dark brown chestnuts.

"Chestnuts roasting on an open fire…" he sang to

himself.

He realized that the nuts would be a perfect surprise for Lorraine. They may not have the necessary open fire in the hearth to roast the chestnuts, but he would find a way, even if he had to build a fire in the backyard.

Charles returned home with his gifts and hid them in the drawer of his workbench in the basement. He was feeling very proud of himself.

A few minutes after he got home, the telephone rang.

"Merry Christmas Charlie-boy," Mike Cooper's voice boomed through the receiver.

"And to you," Charles replied.

"You've got half a ton of toys sitting here at my office Charlie-boy. Are you planning on coming by or do you think Santa will stop here and deliver them for you?" Mike asked.

"Oh geez," Charles said. "I forgot all about picking them up. I'll head right over there."

"No problem, Charlie-boy," Mike laughed. "I'll still be here trying to sober up a few salesmen and my receptionist by the looks of the way the party is going out there."

Charles called to Lorraine that he had to back out to see Mike down at the dealership. His car's interior was still warm from the previous trip when he pulled back out of the driveway and onto Parkland Drive heading to Cooper Ford. On the way, he passed the gas station where all his troubles started a couple of weeks before.

"He rolled down his window and shouted, "I'm never going to buy gas at your station again, you half-wit!"

"Especially if I'm driving Lorraine home from the dentist's," he thought.

Several people on the sidewalk were startled to hear Charles yelling at the gas station. The attendant who had caused all of Charles' problems had his head under the hood of a car at the pumps. On hearing Charles' tirade, he jumped and turned to see who was doing all the shouting. In doing so, he smashed his head on the hood of the car and nearly knocked himself as senseless as Louise had been the night Charles had stopped for gas.

Thinking back on that night actually made Charles smile. How many people other than him could have such a massive confusion rain down upon their heads just because their wife was unconscious in the passenger seat?

He decided that kind of luck would only happen to him, and if he could avoid it, never again.

Charles pulled into the lot of Mike Cooper's dealership and got out of the car. Loud Christmas music was coming from inside the showroom. He could see a group of salesmen all standing around the receptionist's desk with glasses of amber liquid in their hands.

He opened the door and all heads turned to see who was coming in at that hour on Christmas Eve. When they saw Charles heading for Mike's office, they returned their attention to their glasses and the receptionist's ample chest.

"Hey, Charlie-boy," Mike shouted. "Merry Christmas!"

"And Merry Christmas to you to, Mike," Charles said, offering his hand.

Mike grabbed Charles hand and squeezed it tightly in the firm handshake he felt gave him an authoritative appearance.

"Sit down, I'll pour us a couple glasses to toast the holiday." He said.

Charles didn't need to be convinced. He took off his coat and sat in the chair opposite Mike. He took a long sip of the scotch that Mike poured for him. It was a very fine single malt; the kind that Charles could never bring himself to buy because of its high price.

"So, you're already for the big day are you?" Mike asked.

"I guess, Mike," Charles replied. "I imagine it's going to be pretty hectic when James sees what he's getting."

"Ah, yes," Mike said. "I remember when Mike Junior got his train set. We played with it for hours. Are you going to have it all set up for him before the morning?"

"I hadn't thought about that," Charles said. "I think it will be fun to do it together. We can read the instructions together while Lorraine takes care of Louise, Georgie, and their presents, and Doris can be ruining the turkey. Since you aren't expecting me in here until the Monday after New Year's we'll have lots of time to work on it together."

Charles finished his drink, and Mike helped him load the toys into the back of the Squire. They covered them up with a tarpaulin, so that the children wouldn't see what was in the car and spoil Christmas morning. He then drove home, feeling good about Christmas for the first time that he could remember. He pulled the car into the garage and locked the doors.

Lorraine had been watching for him to return. She knew he would need a diversion to get the presents into the house without the children knowing what was going on. When she saw him close the garage door, she called the children into the kitchen. She had a pile of construction paper, glue, scissors and colored pencils waiting for them. Most importantly there was also a plate loaded with Christmas cookies in the center of the table.

"I thought it would be fun to make some Christmas cards for Aunt Doris," she said.

The ruse worked. James, Louise and even Georgie sat down at the table and worked on cards between mouthfuls of ginger cookies. Lorraine guarded the kitchen door, giving Charles an opportunity to return to the car and bring the gifts into the house and downstairs to his workshop.

With that task accomplished and the basement door locked, Charles could relax. He always smiled when he turned the lock on the basement door. When James had been quite young, he had locked his mother in the basement by turning the key that was always in the latch. She was trapped down there until Charles got home from work that night. Now the key hung from a hook beside the door to prevent Georgie from following in his brother's footsteps.

He walked into the kitchen, grabbed a couple of cookies from the plate and went to the living room to pour himself a drink. Sitting on the coffee table in the middle of the room was a bottle of the same kind of scotch that Mike had poured for him down at the dealership. A bright red bow was tied around the neck of the bottle and a small card hung from the ribbon.

"To Charlie-boy From Santa" was neatly printed on the card, which featured Santa driving a new Ford Squire wagon, the same the one Charles now had parked in his garage.

Charles sat on the sofa with his plate of cookies and his glass of single malt scotch. He looked at the tree and all of the decorations Lorraine had put on display throughout the room.

After a while, he went downstairs, locking the door behind him. He spent nearly an hour wrapping the presents he had brought home, plus the watch he purchased for Lorraine. Charles had worked in a drugstore after school as a boy and he was meticulous in the way he wrapped a package. Each one had the fine tight folds just like the parcels he wrapped and delivered for the store so many years before.

When he was finished he pulled two sawhorses out into the open space he and James had created when they tidied the basement a few days earlier. Propped up against the wall beside his table saw, was a sheet of ¾" plywood. He laid the plywood across the sawhorses and nailed it down. He opened a Clarkson's bag and pulled out a large roll of green material that he cut to fit the top of the newly created train table.

Standing back to admire his handiwork, a thought came to his mind. James would not be expecting the train set under the tree. He could have all the pieces sitting on the table waiting for them to assemble, and find a way to get James to discover them on Christmas morning.

Charles unwrapped all of the gifts he had just wrapped for James and set them neatly on the train table. He put all of the wrapping paper into one of the Clarkson's bags. He put another bag over top of that one so that no one would see its contents when he took it out to the garbage. It wasn't the children he was worried about seeing the wrapping paper. Lorrain and her aunt would be mortified if they saw that much wrapping paper going to waste. She'd probably want to iron it and reuse it.

Charles climbed the stairs and locked the basement door behind him. As he walked to the garage he saw James' mangled flying saucer propped up against the wall. It was the solution he needed.

Lorraine looked out the window in time to see Charles pull back out of the driveway. She shook her head, wondering what he was up to now.

Charles raced downtown to Clarkson's and hurried through the throng of last minute shoppers to the toy department. The only flying saucer left was part of a display featuring mannequin children playing in the snow. One of the mannequins was seated on the saucer. Charles tried to gingerly pull the saucer out from under it, but in doing so, caused it to fall over, which created a domino effect with the other mannequins. Charles quickly took the saucer down a side aisle before the salesman could come over to see what the crash had been.

He paid for the saucer and hid it under the tarp in the back of the Squire. It would be the present James would find under the tree the next morning. He was proud of himself for thinking of the ruse.

For the first time in a very long time, he felt truly

content.

It was going to be a very good Christmas.

Christmas Eve dinner in the Kelly house was a tradition that the children particularly enjoyed. It was a buffet featuring buns and cold cuts, small foil wrapped triangles of cheese, potato chips, pretzels and other snacks. There was plenty to eat, a large carafe of hot chocolate kept warm over a candle, and, of course, cookies, tarts, and fruitcake.

After dinner, the children changed into their good clothes, Lorraine put on her bright red Christmas dress and Doris donned her green satin blouse and a red skirt. The entire Kelly family piled into the Squire and headed off to the family carol service at the church. It was an old stone building with large stained glass windows lining the walls and across the front behind the altar.

Doris had spent much of the day at the church helping decorate it for the carol service and the larger second service at midnight. The minister was old, having come to that church as his retirement posting. He could use all of the help he could get.

The minister's son had moved to the west coast many years before. Each Christmas he sent a large box filled with holly bows to his father to help decorate the church. Doris and the old man had neatly laid the bows along the windowsills giving the church a festive air.

The Kelly's took up an entire pew in the church.

In front of them sat the Thomas family. Mrs. Thomas was a large woman. She had barely managed to squeeze her ample girth into her red satin Christmas dress. The seams were pulled tight and looked like they would pop open at the slightest provocation. James whispered in his sister's ear that Mrs. Thomas looked like the back end of a fire engine. The girl had giggled drawing a stern look from Aunt Doris who believed that church was the only place that was out of bounds for hilarity.

The choir had been practicing their carols for several weeks. Charles thought that if they had practiced all year they still wouldn't have managed to get through a line of Silent Night without at least one of them being off key.

Georgie was enthralled by the sights and sounds of the church. He was particularly interested in the holly branches that dangled from the windowsill beside him.

Everyone in the church was standing and singing Oh Little Town of Bethlehem. Georgie stood on the pew. No one noticed him pull on one of the branches. It fell onto the seat of the pew in front of him out of his reach.

The choir and the parishioners moved directly from one hymn to another. Oh, Little Town of Bethlehem gave way to Good King Wenceslas, and was followed by We Three Kings. When the latter carol started, Georgie stopped looking at the holly branch. A sudden look of recognition crossed his face and he smiled.

As soon as the opening line had been sung, Georgie piped up in a loud clear voice singing,

"Twying to wight a wubber cigaw. It was woaded and expwoded, now we on yonda staw"

James could not look at his sister or his younger brother, fearing that, if he did, he would break down into laughter. Louise was also trying hard not to laugh. Charles had to turn away. Lorraine hid her rapidly reddening face in her hands. Only Doris could look at the other members of her family in a combination of shock and amazement.

Georgie stood on the pew looking quite proud of himself. The entire parish was looking at him.

Reverend Armstrong stepped to the lectern and said, "Well, that was certainly a unique solo, wasn't it?"

The parish rocked with gales of laughter.

"Please be seated," he said.

The Kelly's quickly sat down. In front of them, Mrs. Thomas placed her large posterior directly onto one of the sharp pointed holy leaves that had fallen thanks to Georgie's inquisitiveness. Her tight fitting dress gave little resistance to the points on the leaves.

"Holy crap!' she screamed, filling the church with the sound of a very unheavenly voice.

She jumped to her feet and extracted the holly leaf from her backside. In straining to do so, she exerted the final amount of stress the seams of the dress were capable of withstanding. A loud ripping sound told everyone that this would be the last year she would be wearing that dress.

That was all Doris could take. Church or no church, her laughter welled up inside her and burst forth in loud peals. The children followed suit, as did most of the parish. Charles looked at Lorraine who sat stunned and somewhat mortified at the havoc

Georgie had managed to create in the space of just a few moments. Between his song and the holly branch, the Kelly name was certainly not going to gain any popularity in the Thomas household that night.

Mrs. Thomas was flushed red with both embarrassment and anger. She pushed her much smaller husband aside as she rushed to get out of the pew. The O'Douls, who occupied the aisle side of that pew didn't have a chance to step out of her way as she barged past them, stepping on Mr. O'Doul's left foot on her way. He yelped in pain.

The large woman stormed from the church with all eyes upon her. As she did, she shot an accusatory look at Doris and Lorraine.

The minister sat at the front of the church, keenly aware that this was going to be one of those Christmases that would last in everyone's memory for years to come.

Georgie was keenly aware that he had precipitated the bedlam that had erupted in the church. He was too young to realize that it was not necessarily a good thing. Whatever had happened it looked like everyone was laughing about it, so he decided to sing his song for them again.

"We thwee kings," he started.

That was all he managed to sing. Lorraine clasped her hand over his mouth, in one quick movement picked him up, and removed him from the church. Charles followed, as did Louise and James. After a moment, Doris realized that if she didn't join them she would end up walking home.

When the Kellys reached the car, they all looked

at one another and didn't say a word. Their lips quivered in an effort to keep the laughter inside. James made the mistake of looking at his father who rolled his eyes and winked at him. That was it. He started to giggle. That in turn set off Louise and before they could all get into the car, the entire family was rocked with gales of laughter.

No one was able to complete a sentence all the way home. As soon as someone tried to say something, the laughter took over and the words dissolved like sugar in hot coffee.

As soon as they got home, the children raced upstairs to get ready for bed. Lorraine told them to put their pajamas on and to meet her back in the living room after she had gotten Georgie changed.

When everyone was assembled in the living room, Lorraine opened a large box. In it were six ornate Christmas stockings she had made. They were each monogrammed with the name of a family member, and appliqués of Santa, Christmas trees and stars were applied to the front.

Charles was sitting in his chair with his eight-millimeter movie camera and a bank of floodlights, ready to film the children putting their stockings over the fireplace. As soon as he turned on the floodlights the room was filled with a glow so bright everyone had to squint.

James hated being filmed. He could see the outline of the lights for hours afterward whenever he closed his eyes. He was also afraid that someday the wrong person was going to see those movies and he would be terribly embarrassed. He always tried his best to keep his back to the camera.

The children sat on the floor by the tree sipping one last cup of hot chocolate before heading to bed. Doris passed around a plate of cookies and Lorraine took out an old tattered copy of *T'was The Night Before Christmas* and read the poem.

When she was done, she carried Georgie up to his crib and put him down for what she hoped would be a long winter's nap.

James and Louise finished their drinks and put out a plate of cookies for Santa Claus along with a couple of carrots for the reindeer. Charles suggested that dear old Santa might want to have a glass of scotch to keep him warm.

"I think he prefers milk," said Louise.

With that, Lorraine scurried the children up to bed, admonishing them that Santa wouldn't come to their house if they did not go right to sleep.

Charles, Lorraine and Doris sat in the living room for quite a while after the children went to bed. Little was said, each lost in their own thoughts as the lights on the tree twinkled and reflected off the tinsel.

Eventually Lorraine went upstairs to check on the children. When she was certain that they were all fast asleep, she started the task of bringing Christmas presents downstairs.

Charles went to the basement and brought up the gifts for Louise and Georgie. He went out to the garage, and found the new flying saucer he had hidden behind some boxes. He managed to fit it into the box he had saved from the lawnmower he bought the previous summer. Lorraine brought out a package of bows and applied them to the various gifts to further brighten the display. Doris brought her packages out as well. Charles knew by looking at them that they would contain socks and mittens.

Finally, Lorraine filled the stockings with small toy cars, puzzles, candies and the biggest oranges and apples she was able to find at Stigman's grocery store. The fruit was a tradition that went back to her childhood. She was always amazed at the huge apples her mother was able to find for the stockings she and John hung as children. It was important to her that she did the same for her children.

At last, Santa's work was done and his two tired helpers bid Doris goodnight and headed to bed. They knew that there would only be a few hours before the children would awaken and remember what day it was. As she turned out the lights, Lorraine could hear the church bells calling parishioners to the midnight service. Somehow she suspected that they choir would have taken We Three Kings off the list of carols for the later service.

Chapter Thirteen

The Joyous Morn

A faint hint of light etched across the sky when James awoke on Christmas morning. He got out of bed and went to the window. He took the arm of his pajamas and wiped the condensation off the window. In the early morning twilight, he could see that the ground was covered with a bright white blanket of fresh snow.

By the look of the fence posts, three or four inches had fallen overnight. The skating rink would need to be shoveled before it could be used.

He was thinking about getting dressed and going outside to tackle the chore when he remembered what day it was.

"It's Christmas; the single most important day in the whole kid year, and I nearly forgot," he thought.

He quickly put on his housecoat and slippers and made his way down the hall to the bathroom. One flush. Two. Three. Four. After the fifth flush, he heard some stirring in his parent's room. After the sixth he heard the words that signified that Christmas morning was about to begin.

"Dammit all we're on a water meter," Charles shouted.

James smiled and returned to his bedroom. His mission was accomplished. His parents were awake and he was pretty sure he heard sounds that indicated his sister was awake too. Downstairs he could hear Doris puttering in the kitchen. She always got up extra early on Christmas morning so that there would be coffee ready as soon as Lorraine and Charles came down. She knew they'd need it.

Christmas morning in the Kelly household was an organized affair. Before the children could go downstairs to see what gifts might have been delivered overnight, they had to get dressed and wait in their room for their father to call them.

Charles dressed and headed downstairs while Lorraine woke up Georgie and got him dressed. Each Christmas morning, Charles stood at the bottom of the stairs and filmed the children coming down.

It was a tradition that James could do without, because the bright floodlights made it difficult to see where he was going. He pictured himself being blinded, falling down the stairs, and dying before he could get to his presents. He knew that there was no point in arguing the matter. It was all part of the joyous season at 776 Parkland Road.

Charles called the family when he was ready to start filming. The whole procession was a choreographed plan. James led the parade, followed by Louise, and then Lorraine carried Georgie down the stairs behind them. As James started down the stairs, he saw the floodlights illuminate. They filled the stairwell with a blinding white light and the temperature in that part of the house shot up several degrees. He did his best to hurry down the stairs to get the ordeal over.

"Slow down, James," Charles said. I've got a full three minutes on this roll of film.

James could hear his father's voice, but he could not see him behind the lights. He was concentrating on finding each step simply by feel. He knew that there were twelve steps, but when you are walking blind, you want to be doubly sure.

At last, he felt his father's leg as he passed it, and entered the darkness behind him. The image of the floodlights continued to glow inside his eyes, so he wasn't able to focus on the living room.

"Perhaps we should all have a good breakfast before starting on the presents," Lorraine said, winking at Doris.

"Oh, yes," Doris said, catching on to what Lorraine was saying. "Let's go to the dining room and I'll see if I can whip something up. We should be finished in an hour or two."

"Awe, Mom," James and Louise said in unison.

"Well," Loraine replied smiling," Since you and your sister seem to be agreeing on something for a change, I guess we could go into the living room to see what's in there."

It was really just Lorraine's way of buying a minute or two so that she could get her eyes back in focus after staring at the floodlights as she came down the stairs. She knew that there would be a plate of bagels with cream cheese waiting in the living room. It was something that had been part of her Christmas since she was a little girl, and Doris would have continued the tradition with a stop at Mrs. Feldstein's deli the day before.

James and Louise started to walk toward the living room door. Georgie was squirming in Lorraine's arms so she set him down. He raced past his brother and sister to be the first one in the room, a major breach of Kelly choreography. James and Louise hurried after him with Charles fumbling with his movie camera to get the scene down on film. Before he could get it started, the children rounded the corner and were in the living room.

All three children stopped as soon as they entered the room. James and Louise had never seen anything like it. Presents filled the area under the tree and spilled out across the floor.

Each of the older children picked a spot on the floor to sit. Georgie sat with his mother and Aunt Doris on the sofa. Charles took on the role of family Santa Claus. He would be the one to determine the order in which the gifts were opened. It was something he had been looking forward to doing this year.

The first things to be distributed were the stockings. He carefully took them down from their place over the fireplace and handed them to the appropriate recipients. The children quickly looked through the items that fell from their stockings and waited expectantly for the next delivery. Charles deliberately took his time carefully examining each item in his stocking to help prolong their agony and build anticipation.

Finally, he rose from his chair and began handing gifts to each person around the room. Another Kelly tradition called for the whole family to wait for everyone to have a gift before opening theirs. Charles was very deliberate in the gifts he distributed first. James and Louise tore through the paper and opened their boxes to reveal three new pair of underwear. The second round of gifts brought forth new socks for the children. The third provided them each with new mittens.

James was sensing a pattern. The gifts were all pretty much what he had come to expect, especially in light of the new car.

Charles knew exactly what James was thinking, so he said, "Of course, we have that shiny new Ford Squire out in the driveway that's a gift for the entire family to enjoy."

Bigger boxes were distributed in the fourth round. Lorraine opened her new winter coat and tried to act surprised by it. Charles opened a sweater. Doris found a new blouse in her box. The children opened boxes with new snow pants.

"Those will be good for when I'm skating," James said trying hard to keep any sign of disappointment from his voice.

He was surprised by the sweater Doris had knitted for him. Normally she knit in solid colors or stripes, but this year, she had followed a store-bought pattern. She managed to create a sweater that looked just like the one Bobby Hull wore for James favorite team, the Chicago Black Hawks. It even had the number nine in white across the read back beneath the name Kelly, where fans normally saw Hull.

It was the first time James had ever been truly happy with a present that was designed to be practical and keep him warm.

Eventually, the children had a sizable stack of new clothes piled beside them. There were a couple of small toys. A doll that Louise had picked out from the Clarkson's catalog was a big hit with her. James received a board game and a model car kit. Overall, it looked pretty much like every other Christmas had looked in the Kelly household for as long as James could remember.

That was about to change.

"Well," Charles said, sitting back in his chair, "I guess that's just about all of it."

Louise pointed to the back of the tree where two very large boxes and a smaller one still lay.

"What about those?" she asked.

"Aren't those just decorations?" Charles asked Lorraine.

"Well, I don't know," she replied. "I guess someone had better take a closer look.

Charles got up and walked to the tree, "It looks like there are tags on them, but I don't think I can move them on my own." he said.

James got up to offer his help, partly out of following his father's hint and partly out of sheer curiosity. The first box had Louise's name on it. Charles and James slid it over to where the girl was sitting. The second box was for Georgie. The smaller box had Lorraine's name on it, and she looked quite surprised when James carried it over to her.

"I guess that's it," Charles said again.

"No it isn't, Dad," James said, knowing that his father was just teasing him.

"Oh yes, there is one more big box back here, Help me pull it out," the father said.

They pulled the box over to where James' pile of presents lay and Charles returned to his chair with a bagel in one hand and a fresh cup of coffee in the other.

"Let's watch your mother open hers," he said.

Lorraine carefully unwrapped the small box. It was a habit of hers that drove the children a little crazy. She tried to save as much gift-wrap as she could so that it could be used again.

Inside was a small black velvet covered box with a gold clasp. She opened the clasp and pulled the lid back to reveal the watch Charles had picked out for her. Tears welled up in her eyes. It was a beautiful watch and far removed from the bottles of cheap perfume she normally received. She wiped the tear away with the sleeve of her housecoat and cleared her throat.

"Thank you Santa," She said giving Charles a kiss on the forehead.

She returned to her place and helped Georgie unwrap the large box in front of him. Inside were three large construction vehicles, all painted the same bright shade of yellow. The boy squealed with delight as each one was removed from the box.

Louise tore into her box to reveal the large dollhouse Charles had picked out for her.

James sat and watched his sister and brother open their gifts. It was a surprise to see such large gifts. Never in his memory had the Kelly Christmas included anything like that. He was almost afraid to open his gift. The box was too big for anything he might have wished for. He knew the size of the boxes that electric train sets came in and this one was far too big for that.

"Aren't you going to open that?" Charles asked.

James looked around the room once again at the gifts his siblings had received and returned his focus to the package in front of him.

"Be careful with the paper dear," his mother said. "It looks like that box took a whole roll and we might be able to save most of it.

James just nodded, still unsure about what he'd find. He carefully pulled at the tape on one side of the box.

"Oh for Pete's sakes," Charles said, feeling as excited about the contents of the box as his son would be when he saw inside it. "Let the boy rip into it."

James looked at his mother, who nodded her assent, and he began to tear away the paper revealing the lawnmower box, sealed with more tape. He pulled on the lid of the box to break the tape and opened it. Inside was the replacement flying saucer.

"Oh good," James said trying to keep the disappointment he was feeling out of his voice. "My other one got kind of mangled on the Hill Of The Seven Bumps."

"I thought the cushion might make it easier on

your backside when you hit that last bump," Charles said.

"What cushion?" James asked looking back in the box.

"Oh," Charles said, winking at Lorraine, "I must have forgotten to put it in the box. It must still be downstairs by my workbench. Go down and bring it up and I'll attach it for you."

James headed for the basement. When they heard the door open, Charles and Lorraine went to the top of the stairs so they could hear his reaction when he made the big discovery.

James rounded the corner at the bottom of the stairs and stopped dead in his tracks. He had been expecting to find a cushion for the saucer, not a mountain of accessories surrounding the box labeled Deluxe Electric Train Set, all sitting on the table his father had built.

The picture on the cover of the main box was the same one that had graced the pages of the catalog with a steaming locomotive thundering down the track with a full load of cars behind it.

James sat down on the floor with the box on his lap. He was speechless. He carefully read the notes on the box. He had read those words in the catalog so many times he could have recited them by heart:

> "Clarkson's is proud to present our biggest and most exciting electric train set yet. The C210 locomotive thunders down the track layout with real smoke coming from its stack. As it approaches the road crossing section of track warning bells sound and its whistle loudly warns passersby that it is coming. Complete with

four cars, a coal tender, caboose, station, trees, people and switches. Also included is an incredible seventeen feet of track, enough to build your whole main line and a siding using the two specially designed switches. It's every boy's dream all wrapped up in a box."

James set the train package down and looked at the other packages on the table. There was an array of accessories and extra cars and track. It was too good to be true.

Charles and Lorraine made their way down the stairs. They had expected to hear some sort of a scream from James, but the basement had been silent. Lorraine wondered her son had fainted. They stood watching their son checking out each piece and compare it to the instruction manual he had removed from the box.

"Why don't you bring the book upstairs, James" Charles said. "We can look at it together and start thinking about how we're going to arrange the track."

Upstairs, Louise was introducing her new doll to the dollhouse as though she were a real estate agent showing off the features of the home. She started to rearrange the tiny furniture in each of the rooms until it was more to her, and apparently to her doll's pleasure.

Georgie played with the construction vehicles for a few minutes and then, as Charles had predicted, climbed into the large box they had come in and started to pretend to drive it like a car.

"If you don't wike the way I'm dwiving Dowis you can always just walk," he shouted.

Lorraine and Doris shot a glance at Charles who sat looking sheepish. It was clear he was going to have to be a lot more careful what he said around Georgie. The boy was a natural mimic.

Lorraine and Doris started to collect the wrap, ribbons and the garbage that had collected during the frenzy of unwrapping that seemed to be over so quickly. They then left the room to start to prepare the turkey so that it would have enough time to cook.

Charles looked around the room and smiled to himself. This really had been the most joyous season he had ever experienced. Lorraine brought him a coffee and gave him a hug before returning to the kitchen.

As he sipped the coffee, he glanced at the mirror on the wall. Staring back at him was the face of the old man from the cell, who slowly transformed into a grinning Santa Claus. He winked at Charles and disappeared.

Charles sniffed at the coffee to see if Lorraine had added something to it without telling him.

Lorraine was a master when it came to selecting a turkey. She had learned the trick from her mother who always said that the closer the bird looked like a bowling ball the better it would be. It was good logic. Round birds had much larger breasts, providing more meat and less bone. She always sought out the largest bird that Stigman's could get that fit the bowling ball criteria.

This year she had to get Charles to stop and get it on his way home from work because it was too far to walk home from the store with a twenty-six pound turkey and three-year-old child. In order to be ready for dinner, it would have to be dressed and in the oven by eleven o'clock.

Charles came into the kitchen and helped get the bird onto the counter. Doris busied herself preparing the breadcrumbs, onion and spices for the stuffing, which was always Charles' favorite part of the meal.

The two women shooed Charles out of the room saying that he's just be in their way and that they'd call him when it was time to put the bird in the oven. He retreated to the living room.

James was still leafing through the layout designs in the back of the instruction manual. Louise continued to play with her doll and dollhouse. Georgie had fallen asleep in the box his presents came in.

"Can we start planning the layout together now, Dad?" James asked.

"I don't see why not," Charles said. "Everyone else is pretty occupied and you and I can work on this and stay out of their way."

Before they could get started, Lorraine called Charles to help her put the turkey in the oven.

"I'll be back in a minute," Charles said to his son.

The turkey was too big to fit into Lorraine's roasting pan with the lid, so she had made a tent over it with aluminum foil. Charles peeked under the foil to see how the bird looked.

He returned to the living room and sat on the sofa with his son. James sat close to his dad and the two of them looked at the book together comparing the various pros and cons of each layout displayed in the book.

They finally decided on an elaborate figure eight pattern, with a siding running along the back of it. Charles suggested that they would set it up later in the day. He didn't want to get it all assembled and have James change his mind, so he knew that a little time to think about it would save a lot of time later. He also had an ulterior motive for his delay, which would become clear to James by mid-afternoon.

He was excited to see his train thundering down the tracks the way it appeared in the Clarkson's catalog, but he decided to use the time to finish reading the manual and to examine the various pieces that came with the set and the additional accessories stacked on the table downstairs.

This really was turning into the most joyous season for James, too.

With the turkey in the oven, Lorraine joined the rest of the family in the living room. She and Doris brought in a large tray of sandwiches and glasses of ginger ale. You knew it was a special occasion in the Kelly house when ginger ale was involved. It was the only time they spent money on soda.

She turned on the radio to provide some Christmas music in the background. When the old radio had warmed up, the sounds of Bing Crosby singing White Christmas filled the room.

Lorraine took her new watch out of its velvet box and put it on her wrist. She gazed at it for a long time. It was the first time that Charles had ever bought her something like that. Even her engagement and wedding rings were family heirlooms handed down to him by one of his aunts.

There was warmth that filled the room. It was more than just the air blowing up through the registers from the furnace and the heat from the oven cooking the turkey.

Chapter Fourteen

Starting Dinner With A Bang... Or Thirty-six

"Chestnuts roasting on an open fire," sang Nat King Cole over the radio.

Charles remembered the three dozen chestnuts he had bought to surprise Lorraine. The fact that they did not have an open fire to roast them on was not going to deter him. He already knew exactly how he was going to undertake the roasting process.

"There might not be an open fire in our house, but the oven is certainly hot enough to roast the chestnuts," he decided.

He went down to his workbench, retrieved the bag of chestnuts, and brought them up to the kitchen. He slipped them onto a pan and slid it in beside the turkey in the oven. He figured that it would take about twenty minutes for the chestnuts to roast and he would have a nice hot surprise for everyone.

He was right. Everyone would be surprised, just not the way he was expecting.

Charles returned to the living room and sat down beside his wife. They watched the children playing with their toys and listened to James describing the layout he had chosen for the train track.

Charles poured a glass of wine for Lorraine and Doris and a double shot of single malt scotch for himself. Another Christmas carol came on the radio, this one talking about walking in a winter wonderland.

Lorraine looked outside and saw the fresh snow that had fallen. A light flurry continued and Parkland Road really did look like a winter wonderland. It was all so peaceful and…

Before she could finish her thought, a sound like a shotgun being fired rang through the house. It was quickly followed by another and another.

Lorraine and Charles, followed closely by Doris and James ran towards source of the sounds.

Bang. Bang. Bang.

More explosions followed in quick succession. By the time they reached the kitchen, there was smoke drifting up from around the edge of the oven door. More explosions followed. The oven reverberated with each one. The elements on the top rattled every time there was another bang. The smoke got thicker.

"Oh my God! What's happening?" Lorraine shouted.

Charles ran to the oven and cracked the door open enough to see inside. As he did, another explosion sent a smoking chestnut flying through the space between the door and the oven. It narrowly missed Charles' head before it landed sizzling in the sink. He quickly closed the door and held it tight as more explosions echoed inside.

Doris ran to open the kitchen window to let the smoke escape.

Lorraine went to the sink to see what had flown from inside the oven. She picked up the remnants of a charred chestnut that had blown off most of its hard brown coat.

Eventually the explosions subsided. Charles had lost count around twenty-eight, but was pretty sure that the three dozen chestnuts had completed their explosive roasting. Doris stood by the window with a tea towel waving it madly at the smoke trying to push it out through the window. Charles tentatively opened the oven door and faced a large cloud of smoke and steam. All of the chestnuts had indeed exploded. Some were resting against the element at the bottom of the oven. They had an ominous red glow. Others had pierced through the aluminum foil tent that Lorraine had put over the turkey.

Charles lifted the roasting pan out of the oven and set it on the top. He started to peel away the aluminum foil and burnt his fingers in the process.

"Damnation! That's hot!" he shouted.

Lorraine passed him a pair of oven mitts and shooed James from the kitchen. Clearly, there was going to be language that she would prefer he not hear. She suspected that she would be the source of some of it.

Lorraine gasped when she saw the turkey. It looked like something that had been landed on the beaches of Normandy on D-Day. Bits of chestnut shell shrapnel and foil were impaled in the skin. One leg hung limply at its side, having taken several blows from the nutty missiles.

Charles didn't say a word. He went to the utensil drawer and got out the tongs. He used them to pull out the pieces of chestnut that had fallen to the bottom of the oven. He dropped them into a bowl and took them outside. He came back in to see Lorraine trying to build a new aluminum foil tent over the turkey.

She was crying.

"I'm sorry," Charles started to say.

Lorraine just waved a hand at him that let him know that this was not a good time to speak to her. Her perfect bowling ball shaped bird had been reduced to a casualty of war.

When she finished with the tent, Charles took the pan and put it back into the oven. Doris continued to wave her towel at the smoke, although most of it had cleared. There was a chill in the room. Charles wondered how much of it was because of the open window and how much could be attribute to his wife's feelings about what he had done to the bird.

"What were you thinking?" Lorraine asked once she had composed herself.

"Chestnuts," Charles said. "Like in that Christmas song you like so much. We didn't have an open fire, but I thought I could roast them for you in the oven beside the turkey and it would nearly be the same. I wanted to surprise you."

"Well, you certainly surprised me," Lorraine said. "Didn't you remember to poke holes through the skin so the steam could get out?"

"Oh, uhh, well, er, no," stammered Charles. "I guess I should have looked up a recipe or something. I just thought you put them into someplace hot and they'd roast."

She was still upset, but she was also starting to see the humor in the situation. Poor Charles had tried to do something nice in his own bungling way, and she had to give him credit for that. The fact that he failed so miserably was something that would take time to get over, but she put it behind her for now. She was determined not to let a shrapnel damaged turkey spoil the best Christmas ever.

Charles sat in the living room nursing his damaged pride with a large glass of single malt scotch. He didn't want to hear Nat King Cole singing about chestnuts ever again.

With the excitement of Christmas morning behind them, and the smoke cleared from the kitchen disaster, life settled down for a couple of hours of peace. Both Lorraine and Charles knew the peace would be short-lived. By four-thirty, the house would once again be buzzing and both were dreading it.

Charles looked at the bottle of single malt scotch.

It was far better than the brand he normally bought. He just never felt quite right about spending so much more, even though there was a significant improvement in the taste. Now that he had a bottle of it in his hands, thanks to his neighbor, Mike Cooper, he wasn't going to let any of it go to waste.

He poured one more glass, and then carried the bottle to the kitchen. He took out two of Lorraine's canning jars and emptied the contents of the bottle into them. He tucked the two jars away on the top shelf of one of the kitchen cupboards. He took out his bottle of cheaper blended scotch and a funnel and transferred the contents of that bottle into the single malt bottle.

"Let's see if anyone notices," he thought.

Lorraine came into the kitchen and with a certain amount of trepidation in her voice asked him what he was doing.

"Just a little experiment," Charles said.

"It isn't going to cause any more explosions, is it?" Lorraine asked.

Charles laughed. "No," he said, "I think we've had enough of that for one year."

Charles returned the bottle to its place on the coffee table in the living room.

At precisely three-thirty, the bell rang and the front door popped open. No one had to wonder who it was. Lorraine went to the front hall to greet her brother and sister-in-law, a full hour before they were told to arrive.

John looked much improved over the last time they had seen him. Most of the cuts and bruises were healing, although he still limped slightly. His shoulders drooped, but Lorraine attributed that to life with 'that woman.'

Millicent wore a bright red dress with a high collar that was at least twenty years out of fashion. Lorraine often wondered where she shopped for clothes that still sold some of the things she wore. She imagined it had a name like Styles For The Stuffy.

Everyone moved into the living room. Lorraine went to the kitchen and brought back a tray loaded with cookies, fruitcake, cheese, and crackers and set it on the coffee table beside Charles' bottle.

"Is something burning out there, Lorraine," Millicent asked, almost hopeful that her sister-in-law was having a problem with the meal. "I thought I could smell smoke."

"Oh, something spilled on the element," Lorraine replied, giving Charles a look that told him he would be well served to not tell the story about the chestnuts.

Charles needed no convincing on that matter.

Charles watched as John looked at the bottle on the table. He doubted that his brother-in-law could have ever hoped to see scotch of the quality that came from inside it, and he wasn't going to on that day either. He decided to let it play on the other man's mind for a while. Doris entered with a pot of coffee and cups, providing him with an excuse to leave the bottle capped for the time being.

The children came in to join the gathering. James was still carrying the instruction manual for his train set. Louise went and sat beside her new dollhouse and Georgie went back to playing with the box that had held his presents.

Gifts were exchanged between the two families, but it was never anything that particularly excited anyone in the Kelly household. Charles always received a carton of cigarettes, even though he had switched to a pipe ten years earlier. Lorraine received a scarf that she recognized as one that Doris had given Millicent two years previously. The children were each given a cheap, poorly constructed, hand-made Christmas tree ornament that Millicent had picked up at her church bazaar.

Lorraine smiled, but seethed inside. She had gone to a lot of trouble to pick out a nice sweater for her brother and a purse for Millicent, and it bothered her that there was no similar effort shown on 'that woman's' part.

John kept looking at the scotch bottle and the two glasses Charles had set beside it. With his wife's attitude toward alcohol, he would never ask for a taste, and that's exactly what Charles was hoping. Finally, he decided give his brother-in-law the chance he was waiting for.

"So," he said, "Would you like to see what some real scotch tastes like?

Millicent cleared her throat loudly. She was obviously signaling John as to what she expected his answer would be.

"Oh, stuff it Milly," Charles said, surprising everyone in the room.

Lorraine nearly passed her coffee through her nose, and Doris chuckled loudly. Millicent just frowned.

John, wanting to try the twelve-year-old single malt scotch, but also wanting to stay on his wife's good side, said, "Well, maybe just a little sip."

Charles poured two significant servings of the amber liquid into the glasses and handed one to John.

"Drink up, John. It'll ease those aches and pains," he said as he handed the glass to the other man.

John put the glass to his lips, while his wife sat and scowled. He took in the aroma of the scotch and let it fill his sinuses. Finally, he took a long slow sip and let it slide down his throat.

"Oh," he said, "that is nice. You can really tell the difference between that and the cheap stuff you usually serve."

"Oh, I'm sure you can," said Charles, winking at his wife, who suddenly realized what Charles' experiment was. Clearly this one was working far better than the one involving chestnuts.

Lorraine didn't want to laugh so she made an excuse to go and baste the turkey. She was almost afraid to look under the aluminum foil tent. The damage the chestnut shrapnel had done was extensive and she hated the thought of what Millicent would say when she saw it. At least she knew that she could put off that problem for the moment because her sister-in-law never made any offer to help in the kitchen.

Lorraine resented the fact that she and Doris had to do all of the work preparing Christmas and Thanksgiving dinners. She had long ago resigned herself to the fact that the job would always be hers. Besides, Millicent would have trouble putting together a Christmas meal of anything more elaborate than bologna sandwiches.

When she opened the oven and pulled out the

turkey, she let out an automatic gasp at the sight of the bird. The chestnuts had created a considerable amount of havoc inside the oven and the bird bore the brunt of the damage. She tested a leg to see how close it was to being cooked, wiggling it back and forth. She decided that it would need another hour or so to finish cooking what remained of the bird.

Rather than go out into the living room she decided to peel potatoes and get the other elements of the meal prepared so that she could relax a bit just before it was time to serve the bird. She thought she would need that. She also decided that she needed a large glass of wine or three to get through the evening with "that woman."

By the time she was part way through her second glass of wine, Doris came into the kitchen to see if she needed any help. Of course, it also gave the older woman a chance to get away from Millicent for a while.

"I think I could use some of what you're having," she said, pointing to the bottle of wine on the counter.

Lorraine and her aunt spent the next hour getting everything ready for the meal and setting the table. Charles and John spent most of that time talking and drinking the fraudulent single malt scotch, much to Millicent's disgust.

At last, Lorraine called Charles to carve the turkey. Rather than present that particular bird at the dinner table, she felt it was prudent to get her husband to carve it in the kitchen and serve the meat on a platter. At least that would hide most of the damage the chestnuts had caused.

When he saw the bird come out of the oven, Charles gave a slight gasp, too. He felt badly about the chestnuts, partially because of the damage they did, and partially because he thought it was going to be a nice surprise to serve his wife roasted chestnuts. After a moment though, all he could do was laugh about it. He chuckled through the entire carving process.

With most of the adults busy in the kitchen, James called his sister into the dining room. On the china cabinet beside the table, sat a bottle of chilled champagne in an ice bucket. James wanted to create a bit of fun for dinnertime himself.

"See that bottle up there?" he said pointing to the champagne.

His sister nodded.

"Take it out of the bucket and shake it a whole bunch of times. Then, when Dad opens the bottle, it'll shoot some out."

Louise thought that sounded funny, picturing her father with a bit of liquid shooting out of the bottle. She took the bottle and shook it hard for several seconds.

"Is that enough," she asked.

"No," James said. "Give it some more."

James returned the bottle to the ice bucket and the children went back into the living room to look at their toys for as long as they could before being called to the table.

When the call finally came, the children and their aunt and uncle hurried to the table. All three children were in awe of the immense amount of food laid out before them. Bowls of mashed potatoes, stuffing, peas, corn, carrots, and turkey piled high on the platter lined the table. A large gravy boat was filled to the brim with thick dark gravy. There was Doris' homemade cranberry sauce, pickles and a large basket filled with fresh rolls.

In the very middle of the table sat the Christmas pie. This was a special tradition in the Kelly household.

It wasn't the sort of pie one ate.

It was a large basket. It was covered with the brightest Christmas wrapping paper Lorraine could find. This year she had used a deep green foil paper that reflected the lights in the room, and the faces of those sitting around the table. The paper also hid the contents of the basket. Brightly colored strings came out from inside it. At the end of each string was the name of the person whose seat it reached.

The children knew that inside the pie, tied to the other ends of the string would be presents for them to open after the main course was finished and before the Christmas pudding was served.

The tradition went back to Lorraine's childhood. Doris and her sister had raised John and Louise alone, and the Christmas pie was one of the things that they had come up with to make their holiday meal a little more special. In fact, it served another very important purpose. Opening the presents and playing with them kept the children occupied while the adults cleared away the dishes from the main course and prepared the desert.

The platter of turkey and the bowls of vegetables and stuffing were passed around the table until everyone had an enormous pile of food on their plates.

Charles took the champagne bottle from its bucket and said, "I thought we should start dinner off with a toast."

He held the bottle at an angle, and started to unwind the wire around the cork. Before he could finish taking the wire off, the pressure that had built up during Louise's prolonged shaking took over. The wire seemed to jump from his fingers making Charles yelp in pain. The cork erupted from the bottle with a loud pop. It ricocheted off the ceiling and narrowly missed Doris' head before hitting the far wall, leaving a dent in the plaster.

"Shit on a biscuit!" shouted Doris, using an expression she kept for the most upsetting events of her life.

"What the Sam Hill?" Charles cried.

"Oh... my... goodness," said John in his slow determined voice.

James and Doris sat in silence, afraid to look at each other. Georgie started to cry.

"Another reason to avoid the evils of alcohol," said Millicent.

"Oh stuff it, Milly," Lorraine said, checking to see if Doris was all right, before examining the damage to the wall.

Charles stood juggling the bottle and a glass, trying to save as much of the champagne as he could.

Silence fell on the room.

James looked at the puddle on the floor, and said, "You know if we had a dog, he could lick that up."

Charles decided to forego the champagne and sat down. He came to the quick realization that several ounces of the wine had pooled on his chair. He quickly ran for the stairs and Lorraine wiped his chair. When he returned, he said a simple grace and the devouring began.

James sat on the same side of the table as his aunt and uncle. He always sat with them when they came for dinner, whether it was a family holiday meal or one of the frequent times Lorraine's brother and sister-in-law would drop by just before dinner. It wasn't out of any real desire to sit with them. James sat there so that he would be placed directly across the table from his sister. That place made it easy to tease and/or entertain his younger sibling to the point where she would start laughing with food in her mouth.

One of James favorite tricks to get his sister laughing was to mimic Millicent's odd way of chewing her food. The woman believed that it was vitally important to her wellbeing to chew her food thoroughly.

"One must masticate each bite at least twenty-five times before swallowing," she'd often say.

As a result, she looked like a camel chewing its cud throughout the meal. Despite that, it rarely prevented her from eating more than anyone else at the table, or wanting to take home the leftovers that Lorraine would be planning to use for the next night's Kelly family dinner.

James always waited until he saw that his sister had put a forkful of mashed potatoes into her mouth and cleared his throat to get her attention. When Louise looked up, James would be casually chewing his food in a perfect impersonation of their aunt. Louise would start to laugh, sending her into a choking fit. Everyone around the table would look at her, not James, and he would sit looking completely innocent, until his next opportunity.

On this occasion, James didn't get the chance to start impersonating his aunt, and it wouldn't be Louise who would be aspirating a mouthful of food. As luck would have it, Millicent was the first to notice something amiss about the turkey. When the chestnut shrapnel had ripped through the foil tent, some of it became imbedded in the meat. She let out a squeal when the foil touched a filling in one of her teeth setting off an electric reaction.

Charles had just taken a sip of his wine, and seeing his sister-in-law's reaction to the foil on her tooth, and immediately discerning what had caused it, made him snort. Wine shot up into his sinus cavity and he began coughing and wheezing. Lorraine also started to laugh, finally seeing an upside to the turkey disaster.

The first course ended with great excitement on the part of the children. They knew that it was time to pull the strings and find the present that was hidden inside the Christmas pie. The gifts were just small tokens, but they served their purpose. Georgie played with his new car on the tray of his high chair. Louise found a tiny set of living room furniture for her new dollhouse. James was pleased with boxcar for his train set.

While Charles, Doris and Lorraine cleared the table, John and Millicent sat in their places. No one expected them to offer to help and they didn't disappoint by making any movements in that direction.

Lorraine had prepared a hot steaming Christmas pudding with a dark brown sugar and rum sauce, as well as an apple pie, and a tray of cookies and Christmas cakes to be served with coffee. Most of the family was stuffed from the first course, so it almost seemed like overkill to be serving more food.

"Who would like pudding and who would like pie?" Lorraine called out from the kitchen.

Selections were called back to her. She waited, knowing that her sister-in-law would make her usual request, and it was fast in coming.

"I'll have a major helping of both, please," she said.

As soon as she started speaking, both Lorraine and Doris mouthed her words exactly. Millicent was as well known for demanding large deserts as she was for her lack of assistance with the meal.

This time, Lorraine was prepared. A few days before Christmas, she made a special pudding, just for Millicent. She had used the plastic syringe from Louise's doctor kit to fill candied cherries with brandy. She made a special sauce with a rather high rum content for her sister-in-law's pudding. Her slice of mincemeat pie was drizzled with more rum. In all, Millicent's major helping of both contained close to four ounces of alcohol.

Doris was in on the joke. They knew that their target of the prank would wolf down the dessert without thinking what might be giving it its unique taste. Both women looked forward to watching the reaction on the part of good old tea-totaling Millicent as the alcohol took effect.

They weren't disappointed. Before anyone else at the table had half finished their small portions of dessert, Millicent had finished hers, and was scraping the bowl to make sure she didn't miss any of the calories.

Almost immediately, the woman's face started to flush. After a few moments, her lip began to droop a bit and she was slurring her words.

"That waszsh a very good sauce, Lorraine; mush better than what you ushually shlap together," she said.

John looked at his wife with amazement.

"Are you alright, dear?" he asked.

"Never better, Shtud-muffin," she replied.

John blanched, then blushed. That was the name she was only supposed to use for him in the bedroom, and only on the third Saturday of the month.

"Millicent!" he shouted in a combination of surprise and embarrassment.

"Oh shtuff it, Johnny," she said copying Charles' and Lorraine's comments to her earlier in the day.

John helped his wife walk to the living room, where everyone went after dinner. Doris brought out a large carafe of coffee, for the adults, and cocoa for the children. Millicent was barely seated before she nodded off and began to snore loudly.

"I think I'd better get Millicent home," John said. "I guess she wasn't quite ready for the bit of rum I tasted in the pudding sauce."

"Yes," Lorraine said, "I never expected such a little bit of alcohol would have that effect. I thought most of it would evaporate with the heat."

Doris cleared her throat and pretended to look for her knitting.

John managed to get her coat put around her shoulders and he and Charles helped Millicent to her feet. As soon as she stood up, she belched and farted at the same time. James snorted with a mouthful of sugar cookie and began to cough and wheeze.

The two men got Millicent out to the car, which still showed signs of damage from its encounter with the snowplow. As soon as she was seated, her head flopped forward and she began to snore once again.

As John backed down the driveway, Charles turned to his wife and said, "I just hope he doesn't need to stop for gas on the way home. I'd hate to have to bail him out."

Everyone returned to the living room. The only lights were the bulbs on the Christmas tree.

Doris sat in her chair knitting. She had knit for so many years she didn't need any light. Her fingers deftly worked the wool and needles. James wondered if it was going to be socks, a sweater or a scarf. He just hoped it wouldn't be something for him. He was tired of itching beneath scratchy socks, sweaters and scarves, although he quite looked forward to wearing the sweater that his aunt knit for him this year.

"Well," Charles finally said. "It's been a pretty exciting couple of weeks around here, and now Christmas has come and gone for another year."

"It really was our best one ever," Lorraine said, "even if we did have a few ups and downs along the way."

"And explosions," James said. "Let's not forget the chestnuts."

"I think I'd just as soon forget them," Charles and Lorraine said in unison.

They looked at each other and laughed at the

similar way they were thinking.

Lorraine carried Georgie up to bed. He was still gripping the small car he had gotten out of the Christmas pie. Louise rearranged the furniture in her dollhouse and James read his train set instructions for the fourth time; still not quite sure whether to believe that he had really received it.

Charles poured himself a full highball glass of scotch. It was the very thing he needed after a dinner with John and Millicent.

"I had to put up with her too, Charles," Doris said.

Charles chuckled and poured another glass of scotch, passing it to his wife's aunt, who took the glass and set her knitting aside.

He looked around the room, and outside at the light snow falling on the front lawn. He had made some changes in his life and he was happy with them. The joy that had crossed the faces of his children and his wife that day was the best gift he ever received. It was almost a narcotic. He knew, now that he had seen what he could do to make them all so happy, that he would want to see it repeatedly.

And he did.

Chapter Fifteen

Keeping The Joyous Season Going

The day after Christmas was always a relaxing day around the Kelly household. There were enough leftovers from the feast so that neither Lorraine nor Doris had to do any real work preparing meals. On that particular year, there was even more food than usual, partially, because people were still a bit afraid of biting into bits of chestnut and foil shrapnel in the turkey, and partially because Millicent's drunken departure had meant that she didn't cajole Loraine into parting with several pounds of leftovers.

Charles and Lorraine slept in late. Before going to bed, she had prepared the children's breakfast so that they could eat without disturbing the adults. Even Georgie managed to stay in the land of dreams longer than usual after all of the exhausting excitement the day before. The older children quietly slipped downstairs and played with their new toys.

Charles came downstairs at around ten-thirty and poured two cups of the coffee he could smell brewing. Doris had made the coffee and returned to her room to enjoy a cup in solitude. Charles carried the cups back upstairs. He and Lorraine sat in bed, drinking in the coffee and the remnants of the spirit of the preceding day.

James spent an hour examining each piece of the train set, imagining what it would be like to set it up on the plywood platform. He took some scrap paper and started to draw the layout of the track he had chosen and put neat boxes on the drawings to represent the buildings and other scenery.

When he went to the kitchen to see if he could scrounge up a cookie or some other snack, he looked out the back window at the skating rink that was now buried under a few inches of light powdery snow. He ate a cookie and put on his new snow pants, galoshes and hockey sweater.

When he got outside, he looked at the snow on the rink and in the driveway. Thinking about how generous Santa, in the form of his father, had been the day before, James decided to attack the driveway before clearing the rink. He knew his father would appreciate the gesture. He could already hear the sounds of shovels meeting ice on backyard skating rinks up and down Parkland Road.

Because the snow was so light, it flew from the shovel easily. It didn't take James half as long to clear the driveway as it had on those days a couple of weeks earlier when the snow first arrived. Within twenty minutes, he was in the backyard pretending to be a giant Zamboni cleaning the ice between periods at the Kelly Forum.

Charles came out to join his son. He had dressed quickly when he heard the boy start to shovel. Looking out and seeing him clearing the driveway first, made him realize even more that he and Lorraine were lucky parents. He knew that up until then, most of the credit for the way the Kelly children were turning out belonged to his wife, who was sitting on the bed, examining the detail of her new watch.

"So, do you think it needs another coat of water before you put your skates to the test, James?" Charles said, already knowing that the boy was overly anxious to put on his blades and grab his stick and puck from the back of the garage.

"No, Dad," James said. "Look how thick the ice is, and it stayed smooth even with the fresh snow that fell after we added the buckets of hot water."

"Well, go get into your skates, kiddo."

James ran to the house and down into the basement where his skates hung on a nail at the bottom of the stairs. He carried them out to the bench on the back porch, and slipped his right foot into the skate.

At least he tried to slip his right foot into the skate. Like the galoshes before them, his skates proved to be a couple of sizes too small. He wouldn't be gliding down the ice in those skates.

Tears started to well up in his eyes. He finally had a skating rink, but no way to skate on it.

Charles came around the corner of the house and cleared his throat to catch the boy's attention. In his hands was a brand new pair of hockey skates.

"You know, you'd be a lot taller if you didn't have so much tucked under the bottom of your legs."

Charles was proud of himself. He knew that if the galoshes didn't fit, then there was no way the boy's old skates would. On his way to Cooper Ford on Christmas Eve, he had stopped by a sporting goods store and bought each of the children a new pair of skates. He decided to leave them in the garage until they were really needed instead of adding them to the presents under the tree. Seeing the look on James face when he saw the new skates made him glad he had made that decision.

He disappeared back into the garage, while James laced up the new skates. When he returned he was carrying a new hockey stick for James and a goalie stick for himself, along with a bucket full of brand new black pucks.

Charles had never been much of a skater. It was a waste of time that could be better spent reading books, according to his mother. He slipped a pair of toe rubbers on over his shoes and strode out onto the ice.

James quickly followed and was soon sailing around the ice in his comfortable new skates. Charles placed a couple of clumps of snow on the ice to represent goal posts and took his position as the hapless goalie trying to defend against the Chicago

Black Hawks new number nine, James Kelly.

Soon the sound of their shouts and laughter could be heard up and down Parkland Road. Mike Cooper looked out his back window and shook his head in amazement. He never believed that he would see stuffy old Charlie-boy out there playing hockey with his son in a backyard ring that was sure to damage his normally pristine lawn.

James took one of the pucks and skated to the far end of the ice with it. He turned and started toward his father. When he was about ten feet away, he pulled back his stick and fired the puck. It rose exactly twenty-nine inches from the ice surface, which was coincidentally one inch higher than the top of Charles' inseam.

Charles saw it coming, but didn't have a chance to move out of the way before it connected. His eyes closed and he gasped as the rubber missile met his groin. He stood for a moment, and then dropped to his knees on the ice. James thought he had killed his father. Charles thought his son had killed him. When the full impact of the pain reached his brain, he wished that his son had indeed killed him.

James rushed to his father's side, and looked down on the man, who was now prone on the ice gripping the front of his pants, and gasping for air.

"Are you OK, Dad? I didn't know I could shoot the puck like that. I'm sorry, Dad."

Charles managed to gasp out a reassurance for the boy between very tightly clenched teeth. He struggled to his feet with the help of the goalie stick, and limped toward the back door of the house. Lorraine had been looking out the kitchen window, just as the incident unfolded, and was waiting for her husband at the door. He grabbed her shoulder and struggled into a kitchen chair.

"Do you need a coffee, dear," she asked.

Charles gathered the strength to speak and squeaked out the words that made it clear to her that coffee would be entirely insufficient for easing his pain. Lorraine reached into the cupboard and pulled out one of the canning jars filled with amber liquid that Charles had secreted away there the day before. He looked at his wife and just nodded weakly. Before she could get him a glass, Charles had removed the lid of the jar and was drinking directly from it in loud gulps between gasps and winces.

James came in after taking off his skates. He started to apologize to his father again. Charles held up his hand signaling the boy to stop.

"It was an accident, James. These things happen. I think I'm out of the line-up until I can go and get another special piece of equipment that I'm going to need if I'm expected to face slap shots like that."

James wasn't sure what special equipment his father was talking about, but he felt a bit better knowing that he hadn't ended the chance to play hockey with him on their backyard rink.

Charles limped to the living room, and put his feet up. Lorraine managed to release the canning jar from his grip and transfer a serving of scotch into a proper glass for him. She set a plate of cheese and crackers on the table beside him.

Georgie raced into the room. When he saw his father, he ran toward him, and before anyone could say a word, leapt into the wounded man's lap. The only noises in the room were the gasp from Lorraine, a whimper from Charles and the unmistakable sound of a cracker being crushed in Charles' clenched fist.

Lorraine gathered Georgie off his father's lap, patted her husband on the shoulder, and left the room. Charles knew that it might seem like she was leaving with the boy to give him a chance to recover, but in reality, she was hurrying out of the room before she started laughing.

In a matter of moments, he heard the unmistakable sound of Doris's laughter coming from her room, and he knew that the past few minutes of his life had just been recounted for her enjoyment.

He closed his eyes and let the painkilling effect of the liquor take effect. When he opened them, he saw that James had come into the room. He was standing by the bowl of walnuts and pecans on the coffee table.

"Do you want me to crack a nut for you, Dad?" he asked, trying to be helpful.

The sheer imagery of the question made Charles wince.

"No," he said. "I think enough nuts have been cracked for now."

Chapter Sixteen

Back To The Happier Future

The chimes on the door took James by surprise. He was still sitting at his desk. He wondered how long he had been daydreaming as he rose and straightened his clothes. Customers had been so rare at Kelly's Trains and Hobbies, that he was a little surprised to see one. It was the same man who had been in with his son earlier in the day.

"You know," he said, "My son wants another video game system for Christmas this year. People are lining up at the electronics store all night trying to get one. I love the kid, but I'm not prepared to camp out in the mall parking lot. He already has three other game systems. This year, he's going to go back to my past and experience the joy of a train set, like the one I had when I was his age."

The man looked at the intricate model train that ran around a table at the front of the store of the store. It had all started with that first train set James' father had bought for him on that Christmas he had been daydreaming about in the back of the store. Some of the original cars still moved around the tracks and the locomotive was mounted in a glass case over the display.

"Quite a display," the man said. "It must have taken you quite a while to put it all together."

"That's the accumulation of about thirty years in this store," James replied. "I got my first electric train the year I was ten, and I opened this place right after I finished school."

"I got mine when I was ten, too," the customer said. When I saw the snow finally arrive today, it reminded me of that Christmas. It didn't snow until almost a week before the holiday that year either."

"I think I remember the year you mean," James said, realizing he had spent the better part of the afternoon in a daydream about a return to that time.

"It made me think about how kids today don't have toys like this anymore. It's all electronics and video games," the other man said.

"Tell me about it," James answered. "You should try selling these things today."

"Well, when I saw that snow and started thinking about my train set, it made up my mind what I'm going to buy for my son this year. It may not be the Vidsystem 3 he thinks he's getting, but it will give us something to work on together. I may even see if I can find my old train set up in the attic."

The store door opened and another man from the same age bracket came in.

"Some snow, eh?" he said. "Just like the year I was nine."

By the time the store closed that afternoon, James had sold twelve electric train sets, all to fathers and grandfathers who remembered that same year.

James locked the store up at closing time, and went back to his office. The cash box was still sitting on his desk, which made him remember Jill and the dilemma he had been facing about her future. He touched his jacket pocket and found that the envelope with her dismissal forms was still in the inside pocket. He took the envelope out and looked at it. He tore it in two and dropped it into the waste basket.

He put on his coat and hat, and left the store. After locking the door, James started walking home to the old house on Parkland Road. He had lived there ever since his mother passed away ten years earlier. Charles had gone a few months before her. Georgie, or George as he had been called for better than thirty-five years, lived in another city. One thing had remained constant. Coop had also returned to live in his parent's house after they passed on. The two were once again neighbors. Strangely enough, Louise was now Louise Cooper.

The snowstorm that had come on this December seventeenth was almost an exact replica of the one that had been such a big part of his tenth Christmas.

He enjoyed walking in the snow and remembering those days.

As he walked along the sidewalk, through the deepening snow, he looked up at the sky and said, "Thank you."

He was startled to hear, "You're welcome."

An old man stepped out from an alley. He smiled at James and said, "Can you spare a couple of bucks for a guy down on his luck?"

James reached into his pocket and gave the old man a couple of crumpled bills and some loose change. He walked a little further down the street and turned back to tell him that Marie at the diner was probably about to close and she'd probably give him whatever she still had in her coffee pot.

The man was gone. A street corner Santa stood there, although James clearly didn't remember seeing him before. Looking closely at him, James realized that the beggar and Santa are one in the same. Had Charles been there, he would have recognized him as his cellmate from so many years before.

Santa grinned, and winked at James, the way he had done to Charles from the mirror on that long ago Christmas morning.

James turned and continued his walk home. He was confused by what he had just seen. He heard the Santa ring his bells and shout 'Ho! Ho! Ho!" When he turned back to look, he was startled to discover that the Santa had vanished.

The events of the day filled James with a Christmas spirit that he thought he'd lost. As he walked, he started to hum a Christmas song, and then remembered the words, "Chestnuts roasting on an open fire..." He laughed out loud at the memory that song conjured.

When he reached home, he saw the snow piled in his driveway. He knew that he would be spending his evening shoveling. Before he could think about how long it would take to clear all the fresh snow, he heard the unmistakable sound of the plow turning onto Parkland Road. He barely had time to jump out of the way before Steve Murphy Junior sent a wall of snow cascading down beside him.

As he started up the driveway, he heard a slight grunt behind him. Before he could turn around, a snowball struck him just behind the ear and started to trickle down inside his coat.

"Coop!" he shouted.He grabbed a handful of snow and turned to throw it at his neighbor, but as he did, another snowball was launched in his direction. He saw it leave the mittens of his foe. It sailed through the space between them, and stood frozen in time as it hit him just above the bridge of his nose. In the split second that passed from the launch to the impact, James was able to take in every detail of the scene in front of him. He could see the tree, the fresh snow all around him, the grin on the face of the perpetrator and the snowball from the time it left those mittens.

Those pink mittens.

Those pink mittens his sister was wearing.

Louise Cooper stepped out from behind the tree grinning broadly.

"Damn it James. What took you so long?" she said. "I've been waiting here to ambush you for an hour. When I saw the snow today, I thought about that Christmas back in the Sixties. Seems to me I got you by surprise that time too. I think it was a bit easier to throw a snowball then, though."

Brother and sister laughed and threw snow at each other. Exhausted, they headed to Louise and Coop's door. Coop had knocked on the window and held up a bottle of scotch by way of inviting his old friend in for a drink.

"Hey, Louise," James said. "Let's tell Coop we're going to take him to the Hill of the Seven Bumps. It's his turn to ride the saucer down the hill. I feel like we're reliving that year we had snow like this when we were kids. Maybe we aren't too old to relive that season."

"T'was the most joyous season," she said.

"More like the plight before Christmas," James laughed.

A sample from Gordon Kirkland's collection of holiday essays and rewritten carols:

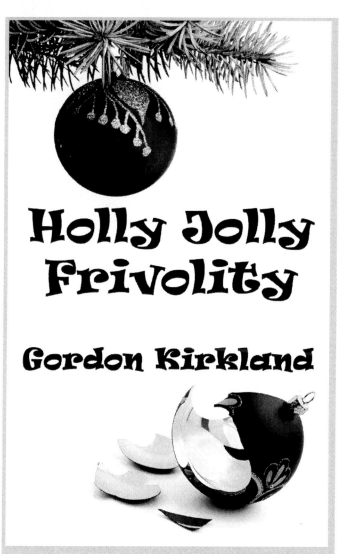

Available in paperback and Kindle from Amazon.com

Do You Hear What I Hear?

I heard those three little words that mean so much for the first time in a long time yesterday. I had been hoping that I wouldn't hear them again for a while, but these things have a way of sneaking up on you, and there I was, taken by surprise again. It's hard to believe that it's been so long since I heard them -- nearly a year.

Of course you know what 3 words I'm talking about:

"Ho! Ho! Ho!."

That first 'Ho! Ho! Ho!' of the season is like the starter's pistol in the 100 meter race for Christmas procrastinators like me. If I don't get up to speed quickly, I'll still be writing Christmas cards on Valentine's Day -- and I may even get them mailed by Easter. Although with Easter in March this year, even that could be difficult.

I don't think I'm ever prepared for the first 'Ho! Ho! Ho!' I know I should be. After all, the first Christmas decorations started to appear in stores when the back-to-school sales were still in full swing. I just want to deny the proximity of Christmas for as long as I possibly can. I haven't learned to accept that the day after Halloween is no longer All Saints Day, it's *All Advertising For Christmas Begins Today Day*.

As a service, radio and television stations should warn us a few days ahead of time that the first 'Ho! Ho! Ho!' is on its way.

There have been a few other signs that the season of peace, love, and shopping is upon us. Like me, you may have either missed them or you were deliberately trying to pretend you didn't see them. Looking back over the last couple of weeks, I now realize that I shouldn't have been at all surprised to hear that 'Ho! Ho! Ho!" yesterday. One of the clearest indicators of an impending holiday season is the sort of person we all know, and secretly harbor homicidal tendencies toward. This is that one, overly cheery person, who announces -- usually around the end of August -- that her Christmas shopping is done. By late October, we've all usually heard the same refrain from a few others who practice the early withdrawal method of Christmas stress control.

How can these people be ready for Christmas already? Christmas isn't even ready for them until the first 'Ho! Ho! Ho!' is heard. They haven't even heard 'Ho!' and they're already at the finish line.

Olympic sprinters should be able to move so quickly. Martha Stewart should hope to be that organized.

According to the recently released Deloitte & Touche pre-Christmas survey of retailers and consumers, 11% of the populations fall into that annoying category. Another 58% have already decided what the most expensive gift they will give this year will be. That's roughly the same number of people who voted in the last election. People can decide what to buy Aunt Maude for Christmas two months before the big day, but they couldn't decide between candidates on election day.

I've even heard a few people talking about finishing their Christmas baking already. We tried that one year. We finished our Christmas baking early in November. Of course, we had to finish it again later in the month, once in the first week of December, and twice more before Christmas Eve. I wouldn't want to think what might happen if I went out this early and stocked my bar for Christmas.

That first, brief 'Ho! Ho! Ho!' I heard yesterday morning sounded the beginnings of the annual Christmas advertising blitz. By nightfall, the television was flooded with Santas, elves and even a Scrooge or two, promoting everything from toys to tools to tummy-tucking exercise machines. Santa, reindeer and dancing snowflakes grinned out at me from ads in the newspaper and flyers stuffed into my mailbox.

It's all aimed at making the other 42% of us start thinking about Christmas, albeit about a month earlier than we might want to. Advertisers also want to show those in the 11% that think they have finished shopping that, since there are still well over

40 shopping days until Christmas, they might want to reconsider some of the gifts they've already bought.

Even though I won't start thinking about Christmas shopping for another few weeks, shortbread cookies and gingerbread men won't be coming out of the oven for at least a month, and the halls won't be decked until after December 1st, I do have a bit of a head start on my Christmas preparations this year. We have our Christmas lights up around the eaves already.

OK -- so they didn't come down after last Christmas, but at least they're up.

We Three Dads

We three dads of teenagers are
trying to make our money go far
Nintendo this and Sony that
And now he has asked for a car

O-oh drive to Walmart, park the car
Swipe the balance from my card
Bills increasing, approvals ceasing
Think I'll just head to a bar

Lego now no longer brings joy
He once was happy with just a toy
Budget's breaking, nerves are shaking
Shopping for a teenage boy

O-oh drive to Walmart, park the car
Swipe the balance from my card

Bills increasing, approvals ceasing
Think I'll just head to a bar

On his list is Nintendo Wii
Next to that PlayStation 3
Five games to start, and accessory parts
And of course, his own car key

O-oh drove to Walmart, parked the car
Swiped the balance from my card
Bills increasing, approvals ceasing
Can't pay my tab at the bar